"Don't knock marriage until you try it!"

Lee's voice was light and friendly as he joked with the doctor. To Natasha, he almost sounded happy about his impending marriage to her.

But as their voices faded down the stairs, she tried desperately to come to terms with the casual way Lee had announced that he had actually fixed the time and date.

He had managed to fit in a quick ceremony at a quarter past eleven, had he? One of the little chores he had made a note to remember: get married, have lunch, board meeting at three. She could just see it in his office diary!

But there had been that light, happy note in his voice. What could *that* have meant?

D0828704

CHARLOTTE LAMB
is also the author of these

Harlequin Presents

358—TWIST OF FATE
364—SENSATION
371—STORM CENTRE
374—THE SILKEN TRAP
380—A FROZEN FIRE
387—THE CRUEL FLAME
393—OBSESSION
401—SAVAGE SURRENDER
404—NIGHT MUSIC
412—MAN'S WORLD
417—STRANGER IN THE NIGHT
422—COMPULSION
428—SEDUCTION
435—ABDUCTION
442—RETRIBUTION
448—ILLUSION
451—CRESCENDO
460—HEARTBREAKER
466—DANGEROUS

and these

Harlequin Romances

2083—FESTIVAL SUMMER
2103—FLORENTINE SPRING
2161—HAWK IN A BLUE SKY
2181—MASTER OF COMUS
2206—DESERT BARBARIAN

Many of these titles are available at your local bookseller.

For a free catalogue listing all available Harlequin Romances
and Harlequin Presents, send your name and address to:

HARLEQUIN READER SERVICE
1440 South Priest Drive, Tempe, AZ 85281
Canadian address: Stratford, Ontario N5A 6W2

CHARLOTTE LAMB

desire

Harlequin Books

TORONTO • LONDON • LOS ANGELES • AMSTERDAM
SYDNEY • HAMBURG • PARIS • STOCKHOLM • ATHENS • TOKYO

Harlequin Presents edition published December 1981
ISBN 0-373-10472-3

Original hardcover edition published in 1981
by Mills & Boon Limited

CHAPTER ONE

"DON'T YOU THINK you're being rather selfish?" Mike's voice sounded cold, and Natasha looked at him unhappily. There was suddenly a distance between them, a more-than-physical gulf that she was afraid she wasn't going to be able to bridge. He had been sitting close to her, his body touching hers, but now he had shifted away on the seat and she could sense the rigidity inside him from the very way he sat staring straight ahead, his face set.

"I'm not being selfish," she protested. "Your idea just wouldn't work. It would be different if your mother liked me."

"Of course she likes you!" His face had flushed and his brown eyes, usually so warm and lively, looked like hard, dark stones. "The boot's on the other foot, isn't it? She said to me last night that you didn't like her, and I was stupid enough to tell her she was wrong, but she was right, wasn't she? You don't like her."

She looked at him miserably, her large blue eyes wide and disturbed, shaking her head. "It never works for people to live with in-laws."

"That's just an excuse," he said, his mouth twisting angrily. They had never quarreled before and she had never seen a look like that on his face until now. She was looking at a stranger.

They had known each other for four months. At first it had been a sunny, open relationship that progressed in lightning bounds from a few tentative dates to an excited realization that they were in love, really in love. Natasha had been walking on air. The days had flown past, each more marvelous than the last. Mike had seemed to feel the same. They were both so certain that it was for real, forever, and she hadn't been taken by surprise when he asked her to marry him.

"Why wait?" he had asked, smiling at her. "We know, don't we?"

And she had laughed and clung to him and said, "Yes, we know."

"As soon as my mother gets back from Australia we'll make the arrangements," he had said, and it was still all sunshine and champagne, and Natasha had been sure she was going to love Mike's mother. He had told her his mother was wonderful, a lovely woman; Natasha was going to adore her. Mike did. He made that clear. Every word he said about his mother was loving.

Mrs. Porter was in Australia for six months visiting her other son, Kenneth, who had married the daughter of an orange grower in Queensland and had settled down over there to work alongside his father-in-law growing oranges. Kenneth and his wife had two little boys. Mike had said that his mother had been dying to see her grandsons and had been cross with Kenneth because he hadn't brought them over to see her long ago. So in the end she had gone to visit them, since they couldn't spare the time or money for the trip back to England.

Natasha had gone along to meet her future mother-in-law on her return, excitedly determined to like her and never suspecting what she was to encounter.

From the minute she walked into the comfortable little sitting room in Mrs. Porter's house she knew she had an enemy. Natasha was not a girl to imagine things. She hadn't needed to be. Mrs. Porter didn't hide it from her. Oh, she smiled and said polite things in front of Mike, but her eyes were icy and hostile, and when Mike was not in earshot her tone changed to a sharp, frigid bite meant to make it clear to Natasha that she was unwelcome.

Natasha had been horrified and incredulous. She had looked at Mike, waiting to see the same surprise and shock in his face, and he had been smiling happily. He could not see, could not hear, what she was seeing and hearing, she realized.

When they were alone he asked her cheerfully, "What do you think of her? Isn't she nice? Didn't I tell you? You know, my dad died when I was four and she brought us up single-handed. We never went without a thing. She worked like a slave to get us everything we needed and she did it with a smile. When I was a kid I never realized just how much strain she was carrying. She didn't want us to know. It was only when I was grown-up that she ever let me see what sort of life she must have had—not that she ever complained. She isn't that sort. It only came out in bits, by accident, and she always laughs it all off, but she's one in a million, isn't she?"

"One in a million," Natasha had said automatically, smiling with an effort.

"I knew you'd like her," Mike had said. "My two best girls just have to like each other."

Natasha had flinched. Hesitantly she had asked, "Do you think she liked me?" She had known Mrs. Porter did not like her, but did Mike really have no clue?

Obviously he didn't. He had beamed from ear to ear and said, "Of course she did; she loved you. Who wouldn't?" He had kissed her, high on the excitement of that first meeting and blind to the reality behind what had been said aloud. Natasha had searched her mind for some way of hinting to him that perhaps all was not completely perfect, but in the end she had let the moment pass. Maybe, she had told herself optimistically, she was wrong. Maybe she had imagined that icy look, that hostile voice. Maybe Mrs. Porter had just had an off day or was tired or faintly upset at coming home to the news that her younger son was planning to get married.

Over the ensuing weeks she had had plenty of evidence that she was only too right in her suspicions. Mrs. Porter not only did not like her. She was determined not to like her. There was an iron curtain between her and Natasha, and Mrs. Porter had absolutely no intention of ever lifting it. Natasha tried hard. She took her flowers and chocolates. Mrs. Porter did not like chocolates. They made you fat, she said. She did not like flowers. They gave her hay fever. Natasha offered to help her get the tea. Mrs. Porter did not like people in her kitchen.

If Natasha tried to talk about fixing a date for the marriage, Mike's mother cut her short and changed the subject. Whenever the subject of Kenneth's wife and children came up, Mrs. Porter spoke cuttingly about her daughter-in-law and the way she ran her home, her suitability as Kenneth's wife, her ideas about bringing up children. Natasha saw that Mrs. Porter did not like Kenneth's wife. More than that—she gradually saw that Mike's mother would never like anyone who came between her and her two sons. Mrs. Porter was a possessive, jealous mother. She not only did not like her sons to marry. She bitterly resented their desire to have separate lives.

In a way it was understandable. Mrs. Porter had given up her own life to make sure her two sons had the best possible life. Natasha could understand it. It was pathetic, it was sad, but it began to darken Natasha's relationship with Mike, because Natasha could not tell him how things were. Mike didn't see it. He did not understand. He was talking blithely about moving into the house with his mother after they were married because Mike felt they ought to look after her.

"She's done so much for me," he said to Natasha now. They were in the park on a green-painted wooden seat and neither of them was looking at the other. "I owe her a lot, Natasha. You're not planning to give up your job, are you? We agreed you should keep it on for a couple of years. It isn't as if we were planning to have children yet. This would be ideal."

"It wouldn't work, Mike!"

"You don't like her," he accused, and Natasha looked at him helplessly.

"It isn't like that."

"She said so and I thought she was crazy, imagining things, but she was right, wasn't she? You don't like her."

"*She* doesn't like *me*," Natasha burst out, trembling, because she hated quarreling. She was not a lively extrovert like Mike. She was shy and quiet and gentle and she was very upset. "She hates me," she said almost inaudibly, because it was painful to say that aloud. It is never pleasant to admit even to yourself that someone hates you, and she did not have a hope that Mike would believe her.

"What rubbish! Don't talk such wicked rubbish," he said, looking at her as if he had never seen her before, did not know and certainly did not like her. "My mother?"

"She does. She doesn't want us to get married."

"Why would she offer to let us live with her if she didn't want us to get married?" he demanded angrily, dark red color in his face.

Natasha opened her mouth to answer and just could not get the words out. How could she say to him, *your mother is jealous. She doesn't want to lose you. She thinks I'm taking you away from her and she wants to stop it.*

"Well?" he demanded, and when she just looked miserably at him, he got up and said, "Look, Natasha, let's forget it, shall we? It wouldn't work out, would it? I think a hell of a lot of my mother, and what sort of life would we have if you felt like that about her? Let's just forget about getting married altogether."

Natasha went white. She couldn't believe he meant it. Their wedding day was only a few weeks away. She had chosen her wedding dress and all the arrangements were being made by her parents.

Mike stared at the path, his jaw rigid. "It's over," he said.

"Over?" Her voice didn't sound familiar to her. This was all a nightmare. She couldn't make herself believe it was happening.

"I suppose I ought to be grateful I found out before it was too late," Mike said, and Natasha winced at the sound of his voice. She pulled at her engagement ring with shaking fingers. They had chosen it together and for days she had kept looking at it on her finger and smiling because she was too happy. She *had* been too happy. Such happiness couldn't last.

"Here," she whispered, thrusting the ring at him.

He snarled, "I don't want the damned thing," and pushed it back at her. The ring fell to the ground and rolled away into the grass, the diamonds giving off a blue gleam.

Mike turned and walked away. The wind tossed his brown hair around in wild disorder. Natasha didn't move, her blurred vision fixed on the distant vista of the park. Suddenly she got up and began to run, tears pouring down her face. How had it all fallen apart so suddenly when she had thought that happiness was hers for life?

It was her lunch break. She was due back in the office but she forgot all about that. All she could think about was the abrupt destruction of her relationship with Mike.

She got speculative looks from the people she passed as she ran. Realizing it, she slowed, turning her head aside whenever someone approached, walking fast and fighting back her tears. Her office was two minutes walk from Green Park. She took a roundabout route to calm herself down, and by the time she got to the modern office block she was outwardly calm, her face set but unrevealing.

In the cloakroom she washed her face and did her makeup, brushed her loose black hair into order and straightened her cream linen dress. Giving herself a last look in the mirror she decided she looked quite presentable. Pale, perhaps. There were dark shadows under her eyes. Makeup couldn't disguise them. But it would need more perception than her boss had to spot that there was something wrong.

Nigel Herries had as much perception as a slab of concrete. He was the sort of man who looks in mirrors as he passes them. He was very good-looking and very pleased with himself. He liked girls and he wanted a good time. Most of his considerable salary was spent on his clothes and his car. He had a sleek red sports car that went, Nigel felt, with his image, the one he imagined he projected. Nigel used women as mirrors. He looked at them and he saw himself and that made Nigel very contented.

When Natasha went into his office later he was sitting on the edge of his desk spinning balls of crumpled paper into his wastepaper basket. He grinned at her. "Had a good lunch?" He did not wait for her to answer. He looked her over in a leisurely fashion instead. Nigel chose his ladies because he felt they would, like his car, go with his image. They had to be pretty, dress well, be envied by other men. Unfortunately, Nigel felt Natasha fitted into that category.

He had been making that clear to her from the day she had started to work for him. Nigel did not waste any time, nor was he easy to brush off. He refused to believe any girl could resist him. Nigel couldn't resist himself.

"You look very chic," he told her, admiring the long, slender legs below her skirt.

She put a pile of folders on his desk. "Thank you." She was used to his compliments. She knew how little they meant. Nigel had a new girl friend every week. He liked variety. He didn't see why he should limit himself to one girl, and from remarks he had let drop, Natasha had got the idea that Nigel felt it would be unfair to the rest of the female sex if he did. He felt it was his duty to spread himself around, however thinly, giving every flower he met a trace of honey.

"Doing anything tonight?" he asked in a ritualistic way. He had asked her so often and she had always said no. Nigel didn't give up, but he had no real belief she would say yes.

Natasha looked at him with her wide, disturbed eyes, and to her own astonishment and his surprise said, "No, why?"

Nigel shut his mouth after a blank pause. "There's a party," he said quickly. Nigel was an opportunist. He never missed a chance. He couldn't quite work out why Natasha had suddenly shown a softening of her usual blank disinterest in him, but his belief in his own devastating attraction was such that he accepted that she had without question. "Why don't we go along, have a good time? You'll like these people. That client who liked the dogs, remember? Fortescue? He's giving it."

Natasha remembered Dave Fortescue vaguely. The agency had done a big launch for him six months ago. They had earned a very large fee for it. It had spread over the television, the radio and the press, and Nigel had come up with one of his best ideas. Although he spent so much time looking in mirrors and wining and dining pretty girls, Nigel had a brain, of sorts. It worked in flashes. Natasha often wondered how he did it. He would sit there spinning crumpled balls of paper across his office for hours and then suddenly come up with an original and stunning idea. That was why he earned so much. He was the best copy writer who had ever worked for the agency.

"Is this a private party?" she asked him dubiously, and Nigel shook his head.

"Public relations—it will be packed. We might pick up some new accounts."

"What time is it?"

"Eight. You could dash home and change. I'll pick you up. It's at the Granada Rooms. It should be quite a party."

Natasha knew what sort of party it was likely to be. She had been to so many of them. They bored her stiff, usually. The people were all so insincere, their smiles artificial and switched off the minute they turned away from you. She would have run a mile to avoid that sort of party last week, but tonight she didn't much care what she did or with whom, because one thing she did know—she was reluctant to go back to her empty flat and brood over Mike.

She lived in a one-room flat in a Chelsea back street. Her window looked out over rooftops and chimney pots. Sometimes on a bright day she could see a few tree tops squeezed in between two houses. Mostly she just could see the sky. She had been living in the flat for eighteen months. In that time the other flats had changed hands several times. People never stayed long. One minute there was a cheerful West Indian girl living next door to her. The next she found herself lending a packet of tea to an Irish nurse with a streaming cold. She never knew what happened to the other girl. People didn't bother to say hello or goodbye. They came and they went.

Natasha had taken a long time to get used to the impersonal face of London life. She had been born and brought up in a small village in Dorset. Her parents and her sister still lived there. Natasha would have stayed there, too, if she hadn't fallen in love with her sister's husband. She had always liked Jack, but one day when she was talking to him she had suddenly realized she felt more than that. She had been shaken to her roots. Luckily she knew she had never betrayed it to either him or Linda. Natasha was a very reserved girl. She was also a girl who had strong principles. A month after realizing how she felt about her brother-in-law she was in London. Her parents had been shaken when she told them she was going.

"But why?" her mother had asked, trying to understand. "I thought you were happy here. What's wrong?"

"I want to see what London's like," Natasha had said, smiling for all she was worth, because she did not want to worry or upset her parents.

Ironically, Linda had tried hard to persuade her not to go. "You're nuts. London's not your scene at all. You're the home-fires type. You just wouldn't like living in a big city. You'll be lonely. You know you can't talk to strangers."

"I'll learn," Natasha had said, although there was a lot of sense in what Linda was saying, but then Linda did not know her reason for wanting to get away.

Linda had looked anxiously at her. "Is something wrong, Natty?"

"I wish you wouldn't call me that," Natasha had said, but she had smiled and felt tearful because she was very fond of her sister and she felt very guilty. Jack and

Linda were very happy. They were perfectly suited. Jack was kind and level-tempered and their marriage was doing fine. Natasha would hate to betray her stupid feelings to either of them.

She told herself that no doubt it was a brief infatuation, something that would vanish once she was away in London, and as it turned out, she was right. What would have happened if she had stayed where she saw Jack every day, she did not know. That had been the trouble. Jack and Linda lived two minutes away and they were always popping around to see Linda's family. Once you start to feel attracted to someone out of reach, it is wisest to avoid them, and the only way Natasha could do that was to go right away.

It had taken her three months to forget her attraction toward Jack. She had worked on it. Her job had helped. It was exciting to work in a big advertising agency. She met a lot of people. She saw a lot of new faces. Despite Linda's fears she made a lot of friends, although none of them was very close. It might, Natasha thought, be more accurate to call them friendly acquaintances. Whatever you called them, they distracted her from any lingering memory of Jack, and it wasn't long before she barely thought of him except when she got letters from Linda.

Natasha was relieved when she realized she had got over it. She didn't like feeling guilty toward her sister, nor did she like feeling she couldn't go home. By then she was absorbed in her job and her life in London, and when she met Mike the cure was complete.

As she got dressed for the party that evening she wondered how she was going to break it to her family. She and Mike had driven down there several times. Her parents had liked him. Linda had been less enthusiastic, for some reason.

"You do like him, don't you?" Natasha had asked. Her sister had hesitated, the barest perceptible beat of time passing before she had said too brightly, "Yes, of course I do." Natasha hadn't known exactly why Linda didn't go overboard about Mike. He was a very different type to Jack, of course. Mike was talkative, lively, very sure of himself. He wasn't really Linda's type, perhaps. Linda was quite self-assertive, too. That was why she and Jack slotted together so well. Their temperaments were so different.

Natasha wanted her sister to like Mike, but within the family circle there was always a hidden form of competition going on, a muted rivalry, a desire to dominate and run things. Jack let Linda run their lives. Mostly, Mr. and Mrs. Blair had somehow let her do so, too. Natasha was far too self-effacing to enter into a struggle with her sister. In the Blair family Linda had always had a walkover, and when she met Mike Porter and sized him up, sparks had flown. Mike was a very nice guy, but he was used to his own way at home, used to having his mother agree to anything he said. Linda's enthusiasm had been tempered by her realization that with Mike she would not have a walkover. Natasha was aware of her sister's cheerful domination of the family circle and it had amused her to watch Mike and Linda verbally squaring up to each other. Linda was far too fond of Natasha to make an issue of it, though. She and Mike had made a sort of truce. Mrs. Blair had begun to make plans for the wedding weeks ago.

How was Natasha going to tell them? She stared at herself in the mirror, her face still pale, her eyes still dark blue with pain. Even if Mike regretted that quarrel, she thought, he had been right. How on earth could they marry when his mother hated her? Mike and his mother were so close. It would hurt him deeply to break free. Obviously, Kenneth had managed it by going to the other side of the world and staying there obstinately, keeping his wife and mother well away from each other. Mike was not going to do that. He had taken his mother's side. He saw it from her point of view. He wasn't going to understand Natasha's side, even if he ever listened to her, even if she ever summoned up the nerve to tell him what he apparently could not see for himself.

She had put on her favorite dress. It cheered her up to wear it. The coral jersey silk clung to her like a second skin, the neckline plunging to reveal her creamy throat and the warm cleavage between her small, high breasts. It was not a daring dress, but somehow the modesty was discreetly teasing, provocative, and the skirt was so tight that it imposed a swaying walk on her without her consent. She had been of two minds about it when she and Mike saw it in the shop, but Mike had made her buy it. He had said it did things to his pulse rate. Mike had always got his own way with her. Natasha liked doing what he wanted. It made her happy. It completed her. Natasha was intensely feminine, a girl whose blue eyes and slenderly curved body somehow conveyed to the men she met the suggestion that she would yield to their masculinity. Her very shyness deepened that suggestion. She retreated in nervous alarm before male advances and her retreat only made pursuit more interesting. Once when she complained about a very pressing young man to Linda, her sister had kindly explained to her that it was all her own fault. "The more you run, the more they chase you. Haven't you worked that out yet? Look at dogs." Natasha had stared at her openmouthed.

"Dogs?" she had asked, confused.

"If they know you're afraid of them they chase you," Linda had said. "Men take a look at you and they know you'll run a mile, so of course they follow."

"But why?" Natasha had asked, and Linda had sighed, eyeing her with despair.

"Because they have it beaten into their brains," she had said. " 'Me Tarzan, you Jane' stuff. Why are you so dumb, Natasha?"

"I don't know," Natasha had sighed, and Linda had looked at her with sisterly contempt.

"You should have been a blonde," she said.

The impatient sound of a car horn made Natasha jump. She went to the window and looked down. Nigel's red sports car was outside. He had the hood back and was staring up, his hand on the horn. He saw her and waved and she waved back. Going back to the dressing table, she sprayed some perfume behind her ears, at her wrists and throat. The light fragrance drifted around her as she walked out. She was beginning to wish she hadn't said she would go to the party, but her little flat seemed so empty and quiet and the problem of Mike and his mother was making her head ache. At least with Nigel she would be unlikely to have time to think. She would be too busy eluding his octopus techniques. Although Natasha was shy she was also strong-willed in her way. She had no doubt she would manage to keep Nigel at bay. His own vanity made him easy to dissuade. He always thought he would get you next time. It is only desperate men who won't go away.

Nigel swung open the car door and sniffed cheerfully. "Like your perfume. Balmain, isn't it?"

She climbed in beside him. "Yes." Mike had given it to her the day they got engaged. Natasha couldn't afford expensive perfume on her salary. Her flat was tiny and cost more than she could afford, but it meant that she could save on fares, and it was very convenient to live so close to the heart of London. Natasha liked the Thames and she liked living where she could see the river every day. It gave her a sense of escape. It freed her from the gray net of the closely set London streets. It was always changing, always different, and she knew it rolled down to the open sea eventually.

"You look delicious," Nigel said as he started the engine and drove away. "Like that dress. Seen you wear it before." The car zipped around a corner and fed into the mainstream of traffic flowing back into the city. "Going to be a great evening," Nigel told her, the wind blowing through his light corn-colored hair. He had a romantic profile. When he wasn't smiling, in outline he looked like a young poet, almost ethereal, his features perfectly proportioned.

"You look very smart, too," Natasha said, and he smiled faintly, not looking at her, a satisfied little smile, the smile of an artist who has been recognized at last.

"New suit," he said.

"I thought it was," she said. It was beautifully cut and gave his slim body a graceful look, almost willowy.

"We'll be a stunning pair," Nigel said, because he saw his female companions in much the same light as he saw his clothes. It wasn't very flattering to realize you were an accessory, but Natasha knew that was how he saw her. Nigel was wearing a pale blue, three-piece suit with a shirt striped in sexy dark blue, a blue tie and a girl in a coral dress. That was how he saw the situation.

The party was crowded when they arrived, and Nigel held her hand while he weaved a way through the crush to get glasses of champagne. Sipping his champagne, he looked around at the other faces, skimming them for likely prospects.

"There's Sonia," he said, and Natasha's heart sank. Sonia Warren was a public-relations officer with a large manufacturer, and she used the agency from time to time. Natasha did not like her. Sonia smiled a lot and her smiles meant even less than Nigel's. Nigel waved and Sonia appeared beside them a moment later. Nigel kissed her and they cooed at each other while Natasha watched and wondered what she was doing here.

Nigel was talking. His glass, she noticed, was empty. "I'll get you another drink," she offered, taking the glass, and he gave her a warm smile.

"Thanks, sweetie."

Sonia absentmindedly handed Natasha her glass, too. "Thanks, darling."

Natasha looked at her but backed away with the two glasses. She put them down and got three more. When she got back Sonia and Nigel were a crowd. Natasha slid their glasses into their hands and stood sipping her own and listening as the conversation swelled and fell.

A waiter with a tray came past and Nigel stopped him and took some more champagne. Natasha accepted another glass. Champagne made her very thirsty, she thought.

"Having a good time?" asked Nigel, smiling down at her, his eyes crinkling in his version of a charming smile.

"Lovely," Natasha said, finishing her champagne.

She had realized another fact about champagne. It was a marvelous cure for too much thinking. Three glasses and she was hardly thinking at all. She stood there and listened and stared at smiling faces.

She wasn't really taking in what was being said, of course, and it was only one word that leaped out suddenly. "Mother-in-law..." someone said, and Natasha focused on him sharply. "Tiresome old bat," the man said, and Natasha laughed.

He looked at her, pleased.

Everyone looked at her. She had the feeling nobody had noticed her before. They all seemed surprised to see her there.

Even Nigel turned his romantic profile and stared at her, as if just remembering he had brought her with him.

"Where have you been all my life, you enchanting creature?" asked the man with the mother-in-law.

"Hands off," Nigel said, sliding an arm around her. "She's with me. Down, Rover."

"Sorry, I'm sure," the other man said, bowing and swaying like an elephant.

Natasha laughed again. She had no idea why. Laughter was floating around in her head like soap bubbles. Someone moved in the little group of people standing nearby and a black head swung around. Natasha met a pair of narrowed gray eyes and smiled into them, a sleepy champagne-induced smile.

"We haven't met," said the man with the mother-in-law.

"And you're not going to," Nigel told him. "Fly off home to the old bat."

Everyone laughed. There was a sudden shift, one of

those shuffles that rearrange grouping at a party. People drifted off. People arrived. Natasha leaned on Nigel's arm around her waist and went on listening and not talking.

"Saw your car," someone said to Nigel. "Fast, is she? How many miles to a gallon?"

"Fifteen or so," he said idly, and the other man gave a snort.

"Fifteen? You must be crazy. How can you afford a car that eats up petrol like that? I get twenty-five miles out of mine."

"What do you drive? A pram?" Nigel mocked, and people laughed. Someone else claimed their car did forty miles to the gallon and there was a hoot of disbelief.

Natasha looked across the circle of faces. The man with gray eyes had somehow appeared in it. He was standing opposite her and watching her, a faint smile curving his mouth.

She smiled back lazily. She felt reckless and elated, her mind totally divorced from memory or consequence.

"I bet my car does a damned sight better than yours on the flat," someone was saying to Nigel, who was making hooting noises of denial.

"Twenty-five pounds says it does," the other man insisted, and Nigel said that one day they must test that out.

"Why not now? Mine's outside."

"Don't be ridiculous," someone said. "What a crazy idea."

"Find a good straight road and then we'll see," said the man wagering twenty-five pounds.

Nigel excitedly said, "You're on."

There was a great deal of laughter, some impatient argument. Natasha listened and looked into the opposite gray eyes. He had black eyelashes that curled back from them and gave them a very sexy setting. He was as silent as Natasha herself, although several times people had spoken to him and got smiling nods or shakes of his head.

He was very tall, his black head above that of all the other men. His light suit was worn with the sort of casual style that dictates its own terms. Natasha liked his loose-limbed, elegant movements, the smooth self-confident way he carried himself. She wasn't the only girl who had noticed him or who liked his looks. Sonia was eyeing him with a predatory gleam and several others in the group smiled at him from time to time. He was the sort of man who walks into a room full of people and gets noticed at once. He had a masculinity that wasn't aggressive, an electric sexuality that wasn't overt, those gray eyes cool and aware, that strong, beautifully shaped mouth relaxed in a line that had an explosive sensual promise, the curve of it warm and firm.

She had never seen him before. He was the sort of man she would normally back away from. Aggressive or not, his masculinity was far too powerful for Natasha. He sent self-conscious tingles through her veins as he looked into her eyes and smiled like that.

"Let's go," Nigel said, his arm still around her, and she came awake from her absorption in the stranger.

"What?"

"The race, come on," he said, pulling her away.

Natasha did not understand. She meekly consented to

his enforcing hand, her brow furrowed, and let him pull her out of the crowded room. A number of the others came, too. There was a good deal of laughter and joking.

"What's going on?" Natasha asked as they stumbled out into the dark London evening.

"We're going to have a race," Nigel said. He was very flushed, very excited, and Natasha stopped dead, her forehead very wrinkled.

"Oh, Nigel," she began in anxious dismay. "I don't think it's a good idea."

"Don't be wet," he said, opening the passenger door of his sports car. "In you hop."

"No," she said, shaking her head. The others were all getting into cars, slamming doors, laughing. Engines began to race. Nigel looked around impatiently.

"Hurry up," he said. "I can't go without you. Get in quickly."

"I'll take her in my car," said a cool voice.

Nigel looked over her dark head, scowling. "Who're you?"

Sonia materialized, all smiles. "Lee Farrell, darling. You must know Lee. Hello, Lee, remember me? Sonia—"

He cut her short, smiling dryly. "I remember," he said, and then he looked at Natasha. "Will you come with me? You don't want to ride shotgun in a crazy race, do you?"

"No," she said, and Nigel looked furious, his face flushing.

"Now, look here, she's with me."

The cars were beginning to move off, and he looked around with an irritated face.

"Come on, Natasha," he said, grabbing her.

She was detached from him with one smooth movement. "She'll be safer with me," said Lee Farrell.

Nigel said something violent. He leaped into his car and a few seconds later the engine fired, the car reversed and was off in a flash.

Natasha was sleepily leaning in the circle of Lee Farrell's arm and past caring.

She met Sonia's piercing gaze and smiled at her. "Enjoy yourselves," Sonia said nastily as she turned and walked away.

"What shall we do?" Lee asked, looking down at Natasha with an intent smile.

"Whatever you like," she said in faintly blurred tones.

"You're all mine, are you?" he asked, a glint of mockery in his eyes.

"From head to toe," she said recklessly. "We could drive into the country. Drive and keep driving all night."

"That wasn't how I planned to spend the night, actually," he said, his mouth warmly amused. "I had other ideas."

"I love the country," Natasha said. "Birds and trees and rivers. I like that. Especially at night. Quiet at night. Like that."

"The country it shall be, then," said Lee Farrell, his face rather thoughtful. "I think I know just the place."

"Lovely, super," Natasha said.

He steered her softly yielding body to a long black car and helped her into it. As he got in next to her and started the car, Natasha leaned her head back on the smooth upholstery, smiling at nothing.

"Where are we going?" she asked as the car shot away.

"We agreed. The country."

"Good," she said, settling down with a sigh. She was oddly clearheaded in a crazy way. She knew she was behaving like a reckless idiot, but she was enjoying this strange sense of dreamlike unreality where there was no past and no future, only the present, and that was shot with golden laughter, bubbles of champagne.

They cleared the London suburbs and drove on into a silent countryside. There wasn't much traffic out here. Natasha had no idea where they were and she did not care. She watched the telegraph poles flash past. She watched the dark blue night sky light with tiny pinpricks of stars. Lee Farrell switched on his car radio to a jazz station. She sang to a blue clarinet under her breath and he laughed at her.

"You've got a smoky little voice."

"Sorry."

"I like it," he said. "I like everything about you, Natasha, especially your eyes. Your name's nice, too. Unusual."

"My mother was mad about Russian novels when I was born," Natasha said. "She was reading *War and Peace*, so she named me after the heroine."

"Wise choice. It suits you."

"Thank you," she said, smiling at him with her head flung back and her loose, silky hair blowing about in the wind.

"You look like a mermaid," he murmured. "A mysterious half-human, half-fairy creature. You don't look real."

"I'm not," she said. "I'm not even here. I'm floating up there," she pointed to the dark sky. "In a bubble."

He laughed, then frowned. "Bubbles burst."

"Not mine, not tonight," she said. "And to hell with tomorrow."

Lee took one hand off the wheel and stroked her flushed cheek with one long, tender finger. "To hell with tomorrow," he said as he drove her off into the night.

CHAPTER TWO

AT SOME STAGE DURING THE DRIVE she watched the moon slide out from behind inky black clouds and show her the troubled surface of a tossing sea. Natasha sat upright, openmouthed in astonishment. "The sea," she pointed out, and Lee Farrell gave her an amused grin.

"That's right."

"Were you heading for the sea?"

"Uh-huh."

"Where are we?"

"Kent," he said. "The downs."

Natasha's eye roved around the horizon and saw the rolling downlands, smooth cropped turf on which sheep grazed, the moonlight giving a silvery glimmer to the traces of white chalk showing between the thin grass, with dark mysterious woods cloaking the horizon in the background, their shadow falling black over the moonlit land beyond them.

"Magical," she said, snuggling down in the seat.

Lee looked down at her. "Warm enough?" It was a warm night, the cool air gliding over her face as the car sped along these narrow roads very pleasant.

"I'm fine, just fine," she chanted, and he laughed.

"I hope that's not just the champagne talking."

"Don't knock champagne," Natasha said. "It's great stuff." The car took a steep left-hand corner and began to climb a hill that looked practically perpendicular. On either side of them wooded banks hung above the car, the moonlight trickled down between the closely woven trees like water finding its own level to lie in flowing pools on the mossy ground.

"Where are we going now?" she asked interestedly, peering around her.

"It's a magical mystery drive," Lee said. "Wait and see."

The road wound around and around, getting so narrow there was just room for the car to scrape between those high banks. They passed a few houses. A dog barked from one of them at the sound of the engine. The windows were all dark.

"We're the only people in the world awake. Everyone else is asleep," Natasha said, and for some reason that seemed the way it should be. She felt that this was a night out of time, a dream in which she was waking, something too strange for anyone else to share it. Lee glanced down at her and brushed some of the flying hair back from her face.

"Happy?"

"Yes," she said, buoyed on the golden cloud of reckless gaiety. She no longer knew who she was, any more than she knew where they were going. The Natasha Blair whose life had come to pieces in her hands that morning was some other girl—a shy, serious introvert who had never skated close to the dangerous edge of things. The Natasha sitting in the car beside Lee Farrell was very different. She was adrift from the waking self, able to say and do whatever she liked, free in a way she had never imagined.

"It's amazing," she said irrelevantly.

Lee said, "Yes, isn't it?" as if he understood exactly what she meant.

The car slowed as it reached the crest of the hill. The road split three ways. Lee took the left-hand fork and purred along what seemed to be a cart track. Suddenly they stopped. Natasha looked up at a small, white cottage.

"Here we are," Lee said, getting out, and when he opened her door she cheerfully got out, too, and followed him to the front door. He felt along the top lintel and produced a key.

The door creaked as he unlocked it, and Natasha said, "It's haunted."

"Of course, it's haunted," he said, waving her inside. He switched on the light and Natasha wandered into the tiny room on the right. It was furnished comfortably but it had the cold look of a house that is not lived in, and she shivered slightly.

"Cold?" Lee asked, joining her. He put his arms around her waist and she leaned her head on his shoulder without alarm. She felt him stroking her hair. It was nice.

"I like that," she told him.

"What a coincidence, so do I," he said. "Hungry?"

"Yes," she said, surprised. She hadn't known she was, but the minute he asked she realized she was definitely hungry.

"So am I. You see? We think alike. I knew we would."

"I wonder if there's any food here," she said, and Lee kissed her ear.

"Of course."

"Of course," she said, because why had she doubted it? Tonight whatever she wished for would appear.

"Come and help," he said, and they found a tiny kitchen at the back of the cottage and cooked eggs and fried ham and made instant coffee to go with them.

Natasha yawned as she finished her coffee, and Lee watched her, the pupils of his gray eyes dark and lustrous.

"Bed," he said softly, and she smiled sleepily at him, letting him pull her to her feet. He held her waist as they went up the stairs and she felt warm and contented and safe. Her eyes were so heavy she could hardly force them open. When she did she was in a high-ceilinged bedroom. Rafters black with age sloped over her head, the walls were papered in a tiny floral pattern, and a chintz lamp glowed warmly by a wide pink-quilted bed.

"I'm so tired," she told Lee.

He unzipped her dress and his hand slowly slid inside it. She found the soft stroke of his fingertips along her spine very soothing. "Mmm," she murmured, her eyes half-closed.

"Like that?"

"Mmm."

He bent his head and his lips gently brushed her mouth. "You're beautiful."

"So are you," she said gravely.

"Thank you," he said, unclipping her bra while his mouth played teasingly with hers. Her dress slithered down to her feet. Her bra followed it. Through her flickering lids she saw Lee's eyes moving over her. His hand followed the naked curve of her body. A sigh breathed through her parted lips. It was all new to her. She and Mike had never got this far. The Natasha she had left behind had been too inhibited, too tense, too self-conscious to let Mike take her over the final border, but the Natasha standing so submissively in the silent little room while a dark-haired man with smiling eyes caressed her breasts had no inhibitions. She knew what she wanted and this was it.

She shivered with excitement and Lee said huskily, "You're cold; get into bed." He pulled back the quilt and she climbed between the sheets, her dark head pillowed, watching him through her lashes while he undressed. As he unbuttoned his shirt he looked down at her and a twist of amusement pulled at his mouth.

"Am I the floor show?"

"Yes," she said frankly. She had never seen a man take off his clothes. She was fascinated. A week ago she would have leaped out of this bed and run screaming out of the room if a man, any man, even Mike, had started to take off his clothes. Freedom was wonderful, she thought. No hang-ups, no problems. Adrift from consequence, all she had to do was just exactly as she pleased.

Lee pulled off his shirt and dropped it. His bare chest was firmly muscled, his skin a pale brown, dark curling hairs growing up from the planes of his flat stomach. Through the languorous contentment of Natasha's mood another feeling thrust, a piercing excitement that made her body ache with a deep heat. Lee walked toward her, a tall, lean man whose powerful masculinity locked her eyes on him. Her mouth was dry as he leaned over and switched out the light. He moved beside her, the brush of his flesh against her own making her tremble with desire, and his mouth touched her shoulder.

"The minute I saw you," he whispered, kissing her

warm skin. "The minute I saw you I got an electric shock. Was it the same for you? I've never known anything like it. It's like riding the surf, a feeling of being unstoppable."

Natasha was too engrossed in her own exploration, her own discoveries, as her fingers felt their way blindly along the muscled firmness of his chest and arms.

He kissed her mouth and she wound her arms around his neck and kissed him back feverishly. Under the heated, excited desire another feeling was beginning to grow. A nagging little voice she wanted to silence because it threatened her reckless happiness. She shut her eyes tight and moaned with enjoyment as Lee's fingers smoothed down the soft rounded outline of her hip and thigh. She refused to think, to halt, to let reality break through the cloudy barrier of the dream.

"Relax," Lee muttered, his voice surprised, but the warm exciting brush of his flesh on her own had become painful, an aggression she had not bargained for, because the desire driving her had not had any place for reality. It should have been so easy, the feverish satisfaction of that aching need, but she cried out with her hands against his broad shoulders, trying to push him away.

"You're hurting."

He lay still, looking at her through the darkness, his gray eyes light and narrowed. "Why didn't you tell me?" he asked, and his voice was warm and gentle, surprise in it, pleasure. "I never guessed it was the first time. Relax, I won't hurt you." He moved his head against her and her eyes closed again as his lips teased softly. The forceful demand had stopped. The clever, experienced fingers wrung a mounting excitement out of her, her body taught new insights into pleasure until it craved the final satisfaction with an intensity that unlocked her rigid muscles.

Lee's mouth breathed beside her ear, the deep harsh intake of his breath echoing her own breathless excitement. That nagging little voice had been silenced again. Natasha had shed memory like an unwanted skin, freed from all inhibition and taking what she wanted, and if the fruit had been forbidden by all that her background and unbringing had taught her, she no longer cared. She had been dominated until now by what she felt she ought to be, what she felt she ought to do. When she left home and went to London it was in response to all her instilled principles had told her. She had always played a submissive, female role until the morning she quarreled with Mike. What she had seen that morning was the hard, unacceptable face of reality. She had loved Mike, that girl she no longer was, and she had been forced to recognize that she was never going to be able to marry him. His mother wasn't going to let her. If she had gone ahead in the teeth of Mrs. Porter's hostility and jealousy, her life would have been misery and her marriage a disaster. Mike's mother meant more to him than Natasha did. That was reality. Reality was the force that had made Natasha leave her home. Reality was the force that had destroyed her hope of happiness with Mike. *To hell with reality,* she thought, her hot mouth buried on Lee Farrell's bare shoulder, and she heard his thick groan of pleasure with an answering pleasure of her own.

She had been on the run from reality all her life, it seemed to her. She had been conditioned to see herself in that yielding female role, to accept the qualities that

society expected in a woman, to be soft and gentle and
pliant, to submit and give what was demanded. She had
not been taught to demand in her turn, to be strong and
self-sufficent, to claim her right, as a woman, to match
the male on her own terms. A week ago she would either
have fled from Lee Farrell or, if she had stayed, would
have been shy and nervous and disturbed. She would
certainly not have flung herself recklessly into the tur-
bulent seas of sexual satisfaction and met Lee's passion
with this heated sensuality.

"It can't be real," Lee said in a drained voice later,
his flushed face against her hair.

Natasha said sleepily, "Thank God for that," which
made him laugh in an astonished way.

"I'm not sure I like that," he muttered a moment
later.

She was already drifting into sleep on a wave of tired
content and she barely heard him.

"Why did you say it?" he asked, and she didn't
answer. She had passed beyond reality long ago, the
lazy satisfied warmth of her body lightly pressed against
him.

When she opened her eyes again she couldn't think
where she was. Her astonished gaze stared at the dark-
veined ceiling for a second or two, then dropped to see a
pair of gray eyes fixed on her.

"Oh," Natasha said in a gasp.

"Hello," he said in a deep warm voice, and smiled.
He was leaning on one elbow, his body brushing hers in
the bed, and she got the feeling he had woken her by his
exploratory scrutiny of her.

The exploration was not merely visual. His long-
fingered hand was traveling.

"Don't," Natasha said shakily, pushing his hand away. She half sat up, closed her eyes on a groan and fell back, her hand to her thudding head.

He laughed. "Hangover?"

"My head," she moaned. "It's like having someone bang nails into it."

"The morning after," he teased, and his hand was back on her warm thigh.

Burning color was running up her face. She pushed his hand away again, shaking with sick misery. She wished she was dead. Her memory inconveniently presented her with a succession of images Natasha only wanted to forget. Had she really done that, said that? Thought that? She wondered as the pictures unrolled like a dark cinematic flashback in her head. What on earth had got into her?

"Shy?" he asked, a frown pulling his brows together. "Look, I tell you what. I'll go down and make us some coffee, shall I? We can talk while we drink it." He bent over her and kissed her oddly on the forehead, a gentle grave kiss, the sort of kiss one might give a child. "And don't lie there brooding while I'm gone. Last night was the most fantastic thing that ever happened to me in my life, and we've got a lot of talking to do."

Natasha kept her eyes tightly shut. She didn't say anything. He got out of bed. The springs gave and she winced, the intimacy of the situation painful. She heard him moving about. He was dressing, she thought. She wished he would go, leave the room, so that she could open her eyes and face the bitter facts.

"I won't be five minutes," he said as he went out. She heard him whistling softly as he took the stairs two at a time. She might be wrenched with self-contempt and remorse, but Lee Farrell was still riding a rainbow.

What am I going to say to him, she asked herself, opening her eyes and flinching from the brutality of the daylight.

She had hardly begun to think when he was back again, a tray in his hands. Their eyes met across the little bedroom. She looked away hurriedly, but not before she had seen the dark brows pull together, concern in the gray eyes.

He sat down, putting the tray on the bed, and reached over to take one of her hands. "There's no need to look like that," he said quietly. "It was beautiful, wasn't it? I know it all happened too soon. Do you think I generally just rush into bed at that sort of speed? Last night was different for me, too. Special. It had magic, didn't it?"

Natasha swallowed on a hard lump in her throat. "I'm engaged," she said in a tiny voice.

The hand smoothing her fingers dropped away. He sat up, the bedsprings creaking again. The silence was deafening. Natasha kept her eyes fixed on the bedclothes.

"The guy last night," he said in a hard cold voice. "The guy with the sports car, the freak who was going to turn the roads into a crazy race track—that's him?"

She shook her head. That made the hammering start up again. She half-closed her eyes, feeling so sick she wanted to crawl under the bed and stay there.

"I was in a state last night," she began to whisper. "I'd had a row with my fiancé, we broke off the engagement yesterday morning. That's why I was with Nigel. It was just a stupid impulse. I wasn't acting normally, I wasn't myself." The self that sat in that bed and wanted to bury itself in a big black hole wasn't the girl who had gone to bed with him last night. That girl had vanished again. *Forever,* Natasha told herself grimly. That was what came of shedding inhibitions. When they reasserted their usual grip, they hurt.

Lee Farrell was horribly silent. She didn't dare look at him. She did not want to see the look on his face.

"I see," he said harshly. He didn't elaborate on that. Whatever he saw he didn't intend to comment on it.

"I'm not normally—" she began, and he broke in curtly.

"No."

"I've never—" she began again after a pause, and again he interrupted her, his voice clipped.

"I realize that."

Her lashes flickered and her face was hot. Of course he realized it. Last night had made it all too clear that she was not promiscuous, even if she was acting on wild impulse at the time.

"I'll drive you back to London," he said. He poured coffee while she stared at her own pale hands as they clenched on the sheet. "Drink it while it's still hot," he said, handing her a cup. "I'll make some breakfast."

"No," she said, swallowing. "I couldn't." She was almost sick at the very idea.

"No, maybe that isn't a good idea," he agreed dryly. He got up. "I'll let you get dressed. The bathroom's next door, remember."

"Yes," she said. She remembered. She would never forget one inch of the geography of this cottage or one moment of what had happened here.

She finished her black coffee, got out of bed and went into the bathroom. By the time she had dressed, she heard him moving about outside. Natasha went slowly to the window and looked out. He was standing in the morning sunshine, his black hair ruffled by the wind, his lean body poised in an angry stillness.

She turned away, biting her lip, and went downstairs. He locked the cottage, put the key back where he had found it and they got into the car.

"Is it your cottage?" Natasha asked as he reversed into the track.

He nodded, his attention on what he was doing. The car began to bump along the uneven, rutted lane, and Natasha sighed.

"Don't be angry."

"I'm not," he said, and he was lying. She looked at the hardness of his profile and knew he was lying.

"I despise myself," she muttered.

He swung his head toward her, his gray eyes glinting like white-hot steel. "Why? Because you fancied me and went to bed with me? Or because you were unfaithful to the man you love?" The questions were hurled at her like missiles and she flinched from the rage in them.

"All of that," she whispered, the hot color gone from her face and dead whiteness in place of it.

"Well, thank you, that makes me feel just great," he bit out. "It's wonderful to be told you despise yourself for going to bed with me. That makes my day."

Her fingers twisted in her lap. "I was just trying to explain—"

"Please don't bother on my account. I've got the picture. I don't need any of the highlights explained to me."

"You don't understand," she said miserably.

"Lady, I understand," Lee Farrell grated, the car

shooting forward as he reached a wider stretch of road. She glanced in alarm at the speedometer as they rocketed away.

"Please don't drive so fast, it makes me nervous."

The speed dropped slightly but he drove without looking at her, his face averted. Natasha struggled for some way of apologizing that would soften his angry mood, but common sense told her that there was no way that made the truth any easier for him to take. Last night the roads had been empty. This morning they were crowded with London-bound traffic and the car had to slow down once they were on the motorway.

It took an hour and a half to reach the center of London, and Lee Farrell did not say one word all the way. Natasha's whole attention was devoted to getting away from him. She sat there, willing the car to go faster, to end this journey as soon as possible.

"Where can I drop you?" he asked as they crawled across London Bridge.

Natasha was staring gloomily at the gray water and started, turning to look at him.

"Oh, Chelsea," she said. She knew what would happen if she turned up at the office in the same dress she had worn last night. Nigel would put two and two together quicker than an electric calculator.

"Where in Chelsea?" he asked impatiently, and she told him the name of the road, beginning to give him directions.

"I'll find it," he said shortly, cutting her off.

When he pulled up outside the narrow house she drew her lower lip in between her teeth, her head bent.

"I—"

"Say sorry again and I'll probably hit you," he snarled.

Natasha's teeth bit into the soft inner skin of her lip.

He leaned toward her, vibrating with angry emotion. "You used me last night. I don't like being used. I don't like being used in any way at all by anyone. You may be justifying yourself inside your own head by telling yourself that you were acting under the influence of the champagne or because you were unhappy, but let me tell you, lady, nobody ever does anything they don't want to do." He leaned farther and opened the door. "Goodbye."

Natasha stumbled out of the car. She had hardly touched the pavement when the door slammed behind her and the car streaked away.

She went up to her flat and changed into a dark, pleated skirt and a crisp white shirt. In the mirror she stared at her face, half expecting to look different. She didn't. The same face stared back at her, the oval pale and oddly set, but unrevealing of what was going on inside her head.

When she reached the office Nigel was at his desk with his head in his hands. He winced when she closed the door. "Walk quietly."

Natasha asked nervously, "Would you like some coffee?"

"I'd like a new head," he said. "Last night was murder." Then he lifted his head and looked at her accusingly. "And what happened to you? You flunked it, didn't you? Ran out on me."

"I'll get you some black coffee," she said. "And some aspirins."

"I need surgery, not pills," Nigel muttered.

She walked toward the door and his voice altered, turning sly. "How was he, by the way?"

Natasha kept on going, sickness inside her. Nigel laughed, but under the laughter there was malice and resentment.

"You're brighter than I thought. Farrell, wasn't it? You're on to a good thing there—he's loaded."

Natasha went out and let the door slam. She felt a bitter satisfaction as she heard Nigel yelp.

"Damn you," he shouted after her. "Oh, my head...."

CHAPTER THREE

SHE HAD A WEEK'S HOLIDAY due, but when she told Nigel that she was taking it right away he was irritated. "That's short notice, isn't it?"

"Family troubles," she said, which wasn't exactly a lie. "I have to go home."

He was still sulking over her defection during the party, but in the end he grudgingly gave away. "I hope it's as urgent as you claim it is," he said. "How am I supposed to manage while you're away?"

"Sara will cover for me," Natasha told him. "I've spoken to her and she'll fit in any work you need done."

Nigel looked sulky, then caught sight of himself in the window, which was bathed in late-afternoon sunlight, and smoothed back a lock of corn-yellow hair, his face complacent. "Okay," he said, shrugging. His glance slid sideways as she moved away. "I hope you're telling the truth. I hope Lee Farrell isn't your real reason for wanting a week off. If I find out you've been swanning off to Tahiti or Capri with him for a week's fun and games, I'll get myself a new secretary."

Natasha swung around and looked at him bitterly. "I'll give you my home number. Ring and check anytime you like."

He held up one hand. "All right, all right. No need to get nasty."

She was still burning with indignation as she left. She was going to have Lee Farrell flung up at her every time Nigel felt mischievous, she realized. He was not going to forget the incident. Nigel was not merely vain and self-obsessed; he was malicious, a gossip, someone who loved to hear about other people's failings. Scandal was the breath of life to him. No doubt he would spread the story of her going off with Lee Farrell to everyone he met, and it would be absolutely no use appealing to his better feelings. Nigel didn't have any.

She caught the train home the following morning. She had no idea how she was going to explain to her parents that her marriage was off. She kept rehearsing the statement, but each time the words dried up in her head when she pictured her mother's incredulous worried face.

It was as hard as she had expected. She waited until she got her mother alone because she felt that talking one to one would be easier than making some sort of public announcement. Mrs. Blair was in the kitchen making tea. Linda, Jack and Mr. Blair were walking around the garden admiring Mr. Blair's roses. Natasha joined her mother and took a deep breath.

"Oh, there you are, dear," her mother said, looking around. "Get the cups out, would you? Not the blue ones. We'll have the bone china tea things today. I like to use them now and then, but when your father and I are on our own there doesn't seem much point, and there's always the risk one might get broken. Your father's very heavy-handed with china."

Natasha opened the cupboard blindly, moistening her lips. "Mum—"

"Is Mike coming down later?" Mrs. Blair asked,

pouring boiling water into the teapot. "Why didn't he drive you? Working, is he? Couldn't he get away? What a pity. We were saying only the other day, your father and I, we ought to come up to London and meet Mike's mother soon, or have her here. What about that? Do you think she could come down here? We've got to meet her sooner or later, and the sooner the better, don't you agree?"

"Mum," Natasha said drowningly.

"Have you got the cups out? You're not daydreaming again, are you? You always were a daydreamer, even as a tiny thing. Half the time you didn't know you were with us. I'd look at you and you'd be miles away. Linda now—she always knew what was going on, quick as a whip, our Linda. You were the soft one. I used to worry about you sometimes. You always let Linda push you around too much. It never pays to let people push you around." Mrs. Blair was buttering thinly sliced bread, her movements quick and deft. Natasha arranged the cups in their saucers and looked at her mother with wide, anxious blue eyes.

"I'm not going to marry Mike, mum."

"What, dear? Get that cucumber and slice it, would you? Thin slices, mind."

"Mum—"

Her mother suddenly put down the knife and turned around, her mouth open, staring. "What did you say?"

Natasha looked at her, her lips trembling.

"Not going to marry Mike?" her mother repeated. Her face was flushing slowly. "What do you mean, not going to marry him? We've booked the church and the hall and the caterers and the disco and—" Her voice stopped and her mouth opened and closed for a few seconds while she looked at Natasha. "What do you mean, not going to? You can't change your mind now. It's all fixed up."

"It's off," Natasha said in a low voice.

"Off?"

"For good."

Mrs. Blair moved to a chair and sat down heavily. "God knows what your father's going to say. Do you realize he spent all last Wednesday being fitted for a morning suit? He'll go spare."

"I'm sorry, mum," Natasha said, holding the back of the nearest chair tightly.

Her mother looked at the pale grip of her fingers. She gave a long sigh. "What happened, darling? You've quarreled with him? But these things happen. Good heavens, I wish I had a pound for every row I've had with your father—I'd be a millionaire. Everybody has a quarrel now and then, we're all human. You'll make it up. No need to panic, love."

"No," Natasha said loudly. "We won't. We can't." Tears were prickling under her lids. One squeezed out and ran down her cheek and her mother watched and got up, exclaiming.

"Natasha," she said, coming around and putting her arms around her in a comforting hug. "Whatever is it? What's it all about?"

Natasha burst into tears and sobbed it all out while her mother patted her back as though she were six and listened, exclaiming.

"You're sure you haven't imagined it?" she asked once, and Natasha lifted her wet face and looked at her.

"I wish I had. She hides it from Mike but she doesn't bother with me. She wants me to know. I'm an interloper, I'm not wanted, I'm taking him away from her."

"Oh, dear, I don't like the sound of that," Mrs. Blair said, so comically that Natasha began to laugh and her mother said, "Hysteria," to herself, frowning.

"No," Natasha said, trying to stop laughing, the tears running down her face.

Mrs. Blair took her head and shook it gently. "Stop it, there's a good girl."

Natasha couldn't stop. Mrs. Blair eyed her anxiously for a moment as the tears and laughter rose into wild crescendo, then she briskly slapped her face and it all stopped. Natasha took a stunned breath.

"I'm sorry, darling," her mother said. "Now, I think the best thing would be for you to go to bed with a cup of tea and some aspirins."

"Oh, mum," Natasha said, rubbing a hand across her tearstained face. "You're so funny."

"I'll tell your father and Linda and Jack. You just get some rest and stop worrying."

They went upstairs. The others were still in the garden. Natasha heard their voices, laughter breaking out, as they wandered around.

Mrs. Blair drew the curtains and the room grew shadowy. Natasha curled up under the quilt. "I'm sorry, mum, about all the arrangements and dad's morning suit."

"Never mind, what can't be cured must be endured," Mrs. Blair told her. "Drink your tea and take the aspirins and get to sleep."

Natasha had slept last night for a few hours, but ever since the night she spent with Lee Farrell she had been sleeping badly and she was very tired now, both bodily and mentally, the relief of having broken it to her mother leaving her feeling dead and drained. She drank her tea and took the pills and closed her eyes. Sleep came before she had expected it.

When she woke up it was gray dawn. She tiptoed over and drew the curtains and watched the morning streaks of pink appear along the horizon.

When she crept down to the kitchen she heard sounds, the clinking of cups, the singing of the kettle. Natasha opened the door, but it was her father who looked around at her. He was in pajamas and dressing gown, his gray hair a tousled quiff. Natasha looked nervously at him and he smiled.

"All right, come in, don't look like someone who's been caught redhanded. I'll forgive you; thousands wouldn't."

She went in and stood looking at him. "I'm sorry to have loused it all up for you and mum."

"What? A few arrangements? Forget it. At least you've got the sense to know better than to go ahead and get married with that sort of problem on your hands."

"I would have done," Natasha admitted wearily. "I very nearly did. It was only when Mike insisted that we must live with her after the marriage that I saw it wouldn't work."

"It never does," her father said, shaking his head. "But surely Mike must know she's so possessive?"

Natasha shrugged. "He said I imagined it. He said she liked me, and it was me who didn't like her."

Her father looked at her shrewdly, searching her face. "He couldn't be right, darling? Tell me if he was— there's no reason why you should like her if you just can't, but don't lie about it."

"I'm not. I wanted to like her. But how can you like someone who looks at you with hatred every time you see them?" She sighed. "And it isn't just Mike. You should hear her talk about Kenneth's wife. The poor girl can't do a thing right. I've a shrewd idea that's why Kenneth and his wife stay in Australia. They don't want to see his mother."

"Poor Mike," her father said slowly. "If he really doesn't know he is probably very miserable himself at the moment."

Natasha looked at him, frowning. "Yes," she said. "I'd thought that myself. And, dad, the worst is—there'll never be a chance his mother will like any girl he takes home."

"Unless he meets someone tougher than his mother," Mr. Blair said. "That's his only hope. I can't see our Linda letting herself be cold-shouldered out of a marriage she really wanted."

Natasha gave a long sigh. "No, neither can I. But I'm not the type to take Mrs. Porter on."

Perhaps, she thought, that was what she had been trying to do that night—act with decision, more aggression, more courage. She had channeled it all the wrong way, though. She had seized the nerve to do as she pleased and gone off with Lee Farrell when what she should have done was go around to see Mike and tell him exactly why she didn't like his mother and why he had to choose between the two of them.

Even if she had, though, her brief rebellion would have fizzled out. She would never be able to face a future dominated by a long tug of war between herself and Mrs. Porter over Mike. What sort of life would that be?

Her father patted her cheek roughly. "No, you're not the type," he agreed with affection. "You're better off out of it."

Linda was even more vocal in her views. "You ought to go around and sort out the woman. I would," she told Natasha furiously. "You're not going to let her walk all over you, are you? Fight for him. Where's your guts, Natty?"

"Don't call me that," Natasha appealed. "Tasha I can stand, but not Natty, please, Linda."

"If you loved Mike you'd fight for him," Linda insisted, undeterred. "Selfish old—"

"Linda!" Mr. Blair said, and Linda made a face at him.

"Well, isn't she? Poor Mike, although if he had an ounce of intelligence he'd see what has been going on under his nose and tell his mother where to go."

"It isn't easy for him," Natasha said. "She's sacrificed herself for him."

"And she makes sure he never forgets it," Linda said scathingly. "She's not daft, is she? She doesn't want to be left alone, don't you see that? If Mike marries you his mother will have to build up a new life for herself and she doesn't want to."

Natasha didn't want to talk about it anymore. "I've made up my mind," she said. "I just want to forget it."

"That's right, dear," her mother said. "I think you're very wise. It sounds to me as if you've had a lucky escape."

Linda started to talk again and Mrs. Blair looked sternly at her. "That's enough of that. We've said more than enough. Let's hear no more of it."

It wasn't often that Mrs. Blair put her foot down, but

when she did Linda accepted it. With a grimace she shrugged, and the subject was dropped.

The week passed too quickly for Natasha, who was not eager to go back to London. Jack drove her to the station and carried her case onto the platform for her. He looked down at her with a concerned expression.

"You're pale. Sure you want to go?"

"Sure," she said, meaning she was sure she didn't but she had no choice but to go back, at least for the moment.

"Look after yourself," Jack said in an embarrassed way. She realized with a shock that his brown hair was beginning to show streaks of gray. It was hard to remember the weeks when she had thought herself in love with him. It had all been so real, so painful and so brief. Emotion was like water. It ran through your fingers and drained into the sand of time, but while you held it you held life itself. Natasha was grateful that she had had the sense to bolt away from her infatuation for Jack. She had nothing now to reproach herself with. If only she had not gone off with Lee Farrell the other night! She would not now be aching with self-contempt and misery because of her own folly. Why hadn't she remembered the lesson she had learned over Jack? It is much wiser to run, she thought. There can be no consequences then.

She leaned out of the window and waved and Jack waved back, a faint frown on his face. He was fond of her and he had no idea she had once been enough in love with him to run away from him. If she had ever let him see it there would be a barrier between them now.

When she got to her flat there was a note on the mat. It had been pushed under the door. She recognized

Mike's writing. For a moment she almost tore it up unread, then she opened it and ran her eye over the hurriedly scribbled words.

He had rung her a number of times, it said, and got no reply, and he had been around but found her out. He had to see her, to talk to her. He was going up to Manchester for a fortnight for his firm. When he got back he would call again. They must talk, he ended.

Natasha screwed the paper up and flung it into the waste bin. Whatever he had to say, she knew it was no use.

A week later she was watching television at home when her mind suddenly went blank. It went blank because she had just looked into the newspaper to check the time of some program and as she flipped the pages over her eye had caught the date. She sat for a second transfixed in shock. Then she leaped up and found her diary. Her fingers shook as she turned the pages. She stared at the page, her face turning white.

"Oh, no," she whispered. She counted aloud. She counted again. There was no mistake. She had missed a period. It was four days overdue. She made herself sit down and stop getting into a panic. There could be a simple reason for it. She was still very upset. Emotional upsets could have caused the delay. She had often had that sort of problem in her teens. She was highly strung, her doctor had told her, prone to disturbances in her monthly cycle whenever she was distressed. Those disturbances had lessened as she grew out of her teens, though, and she couldn't convince herself that that was the explanation now.

She tried, though. She tried hard over the next week.

The waiting nearly drove her crazy. She couldn't sleep, couldn't eat, couldn't concentrate at work.

"What's the matter with you? In love?" Nigel sneered, tossing back his light hair. "Can we have some of your attention? Thank you."

She wanted to scream but she kept on smiling. What else could she do?

She didn't dare confide in anyone or ask advice. Her friends in the office were not close. They were passing ships in the night, temporary acquaintances whom only circumstances made friends. Natasha dared not tell any of them what was on her mind. In the end she forced herself to make certain. She had a test and within twenty-four hours she knew for sure. She was pregnant.

She hadn't even imagined any such consequences. It hadn't entered her head. She had been so caught up in her misery over Mike, in her shame and self-contempt over spending the night with a stranger, that she hadn't moved any further into the realm of cause and effect.

She sat in her flat in the silence and felt like a small trapped animal.

What was she going to do? For one brief instant she considered abortion, but no sooner had the idea entered her head than she dismissed it even more rapidly. Natasha had a deeply ingrained moral sense. She would rather kill herself than kill another living entity, especially a baby, her baby. She might not want it. She did not want it. But it was a fact, it was alive, and Natasha shuddered away from any notion of ending its life.

She would have to have the baby. Once she had faced that fact she had a whole string of others to face. She wasn't going to be able to hide her pregnancy. Sooner or later her family would find out, her firm would find out, the whole world would find out. They said love and a cough couldn't be hidden. That applied even more to a baby.

She covered her white face with her trembling hands. She couldn't face the thought of telling her parents. They were loving, warm parents, but they were the people who had beaten that set of moral values into her head and she didn't need telling exactly how they would react to her news. They would be ashamed, horrified, shocked. If she had come to them and told them she was having a baby by Mike they might have been embarrassed and distressed but they would probably have forgiven her because she was going to marry Mike, she loved Mike. But when she told them she didn't know a thing about the father, she only knew his name, had only met him once—they would look at her in a way that would make her want to crawl away into a dark hole.

She spent all night sitting there, going over it again and again, looking into a dark future with no ray of light in it, lost in a despair that was made worse by the knowledge that she only had herself to blame. She had no excuses, no way of softening her case.

In the morning she was hollow-eyed and very pale. It was a Sunday. The milkman was late. She heard the chink of his bottles in the street. Across the landing her neighbor's radio was blaring nonstop pop music. Someone somewhere was shouting at someone else. Natasha put her hands over her ears. Lack of sleep and mental distress were making her so much on edge that for a moment she thought of walking down to the river and leaping into the cold gray waters. Even that was denied her.

Her whole mind closed off that avenue of escape. She looked at the London rooftops and wondered how she was going to get through the next few months.

A knock at the door made her jump. She hesitated and it came again, louder. Natasha reluctantly went to open the door and felt a shock of pain as she looked at Mike.

He was almost as pale as herself and his eyes had shadows under them.

"Hello," he said, uneasy hesitation in his voice.

Natasha blocked the door. "There's no point, Mike," she said to him wearily.

"I've got to talk to you."

"There's nothing to say." Even if he had come to tell her that he chose her, not his mother, there was no way back now. She had closed off all the exits herself by her night of folly.

"Darling," Mike said with a pleading smile, and tears ran into her eyes.

He was inside the flat and holding her in a flash. Natasha laid her head on his shoulder and tried to stop crying. His hand rubbed over her head as though she were a nervous dog and he whispered her name against her hair. "Don't, don't cry like that, I'm sorry. Natasha, darling, don't."

She choked back the sobs and ran a hand over her face, looking at him, firmly pulling away.

"It's no good, Mike."

"Can't we work it out? I love you," he said. "Maybe if we gave it more time? You don't know my mother. If you just tried to—"

Natasha had been screwing up her courage to tell him but the words were jammed inside her head and she couldn't get them out. She stood very stiffly, her hands clenched. "I'm pregnant," she said, and there was a long dazed silence.

"What did you say?" Mike whispered, his face turning a strange shade of off-white.

"The day we broke off our engagement I went to a party and got drunk and ended up in bed with someone and I'm pregnant." She recited the stark bitter facts with a flat absence of emotion that was bred of all the hours when she had tried to bring herself to think of a way of telling her family. She had seen then that this was the only way. She would just have to say it aloud, make herself put it simply, not wrap it up prettily in a cloudy tissue of excuses and explanations.

Mike was staring at her, his mouth open. Dark red color filled his face.

"Who was it?" he burst out rawly. "Who?"

"I can't tell you that." She did not want to involve Lee Farrell in it. He wasn't responsible. No doubt he had imagined she would be prepared for such an eventuality. These days men seemed to think a woman was responsible for such precautions. It was so convenient for them. It left them free to enjoy themselves.

Mike shot forward and grabbed her shoulders and shook her roughly, his face barbaric in rage. "Who? Who? Tell me, damn you!"

"I can't. I won't." She felt dizzy, her head spinning as he moved her backward and forward as if she was a rag doll.

"I want to know," he said bitterly. "How could you? My God, how could you?"

"I'm sorry. I don't know. Oh, don't look at me like that," she said, shivering.

"Herries," he said suddenly, his hands tightening. "Herries. It was him, wasn't it? He always fancied you. It was Herries, wasn't it?"

"No," she said hurriedly, horrified. "No, it wasn't."

Mike pushed her from him with a gesture of rage and contempt. "When I get my hands on him I'll spoil that pretty face of his for life."

She ran after him as he went storming toward the door. "Mike, don't, don't talk to Nigel, don't tell him, Mike, please."

He shoved her out of the way. The door slammed. Natasha stood staring at it. He would go to Nigel and accuse him and now it wasn't possible to hide anything. She would have to give notice. She couldn't stay at the office now. She shuddered, imagining Nigel's face when Mike arrived with his angry accusations, imagining the amused, fascinated expression, the questions, the raised eyebrows. Nigel wouldn't be shocked or horrified. He would merely be delighted. Scandal always fascinated him. Natasha had no wish to find herself the object of a curious, interested battery of eyes every time she walked through the office.

Her choices were being limited bit by bit. She dared not go home because that would cause such embarrassment to her family. She couldn't go on working at the agency because they all knew her and she couldn't face them. She was going to have to find a new flat, a new job, a way of managing by herself to have the baby and keep it and herself without help, and she didn't have a clue how she was going to do it.

She sat and remembered the night it all happened, her own elated champagne-induced sense of freedom. The bubble had burst, all right. She had fallen out of the sky and landed with a bone-breaking thud.

She had seemed to have worked it all out that night, though. She had felt strong, confident, free. It had been a fantastic feeling. She could do with some of that now. She could do with some champagne. The thick gray fog of depression that was hanging around her was lethal.

It was going to take a lot of strength of mind, of will, of purpose to have the baby and bring it up single-handed. Natasha did not know if she had the sort of nerve it would take. She had gambled the night she met Lee Farrell and she had lost far more than she had even realized. She didn't know how she was going to cope with the consequences of her wild gamble, but she sat in her flat with a white face and told herself that somehow she was going to do just that. She was going to get across this dangerously high fence somehow or crash in the attempt.

CHAPTER FOUR

NATASHA REFUSED TO SIT THERE all day brooding. She changed into a pair of jeans and a blue shirt and went out for a walk along the river. The Thames ran restlessly, the surface whipped by the wind into tiny broken white waves, the moored barges tossing to and fro, the trees bending backward and forward with a creaking sound that made her look up, frowning, as she remembered the sound of the cottage door opening and Lee Farrell saying with a smile, "Of course it's haunted." It always would be now, for her.

When she got back to her flat her face had a wind-flushed healthy glow, her hair was disheveled, and she was feeling far more optimistic. It was absurd, of course, because nothing had altered during her walk. The facts remained the same. Only her mood had changed.

She climbed the stairs and met her neighbor, the nurse, who said cheerfully, "Hello, how are you then? Great day, isn't it? And I'm off duty, thank the Lord."

Natasha smiled. "Been busy?"

"Busy? You've got to be joking. We've been so busy I've hardly been able to remember my own name at times."

"Make the most of your day off, then," Natasha said. "It's a nice day for a walk."

"Walk? Not me," said the nurse with a horrified expression. "I do all the walking I need around the wards." She shook her head vigorously. "No, I'm going to watch the telly this afternoon with my feet up."

Someone was coming up the stairs and, smiling with amusement still, Natasha glanced around. Her heart stopped, and then began to race painfully, as she recognized Lee Farrell. The nurse looked at him briefly then her head swung around in a double take, her mouth dropping open at his good looks.

Natasha turned away and nervously inserted her key in her lock. She got the door open and was sliding inside the flat when Lee Farrell loomed behind her. He was in before Natasha could stop him and with the other girl standing outside, staring in fascination, she couldn't make a scene. She had to let him walk in and close the door.

Her blue eyes lifted anxiously to his face, her mouth suddenly dry with apprehension.

He looked at her savagely. "I've just had a visitor," he bit out.

"A visitor?" Her mind wasn't working. She stammered the question as she stared at his dark, frowning features.

"Don't play the innocent with me. It won't wash."

Natasha absently put a hand to her hair, smoothing it down over her shoulders. "What are you talking about? What are you doing here? I don't want—"

"What you want is a matter of speculation, I'd say," he broke in harshly, and she stared at him in complete bewilderment.

"What?"

"I thought I was way past the stage of being taken in

by a pair of big blue eyes,'' he informed her through his teeth. "It just shows you—you're never as smart as you thought you were."

Natasha had the feeling she had missed something in this conversation. She felt like someone who has come in on the second act of a play and is trying to pick up clues to what happened in the first act. Her forehead creased, she said slowly, "Maybe it would help if we started again. What are you doing here, Mr. Farrell?"

"You don't know, of course," he said in a tone heavy with the force of an inexplicable anger.

Natasha shook her head patiently. "I have no idea."

He laughed. Well, she thought, staring at him, it was presumably meant to be a laugh. It was a rather ugly noise and she did not like it, the raw anger in it made it unpleasant and threatening.

He was looking at her with hard, cold gray eyes that flicked up and down and left her feeling rather sick. He had been very angry the morning he drove her back to London, but the anger had not had this savage quality. There was something new in his anger today, something she did not understand.

He shrugged, shoving his hands into his pockets. "All right, if you want to play games, let's play them. I'll tell you and you can pretend you don't know what I'm talking about, but we both know you do, don't we?"

Natasha was beginning to feel resentful. "If you say so," she muttered.

"What?" he snarled, leaning toward her, his long body tense with rage.

She looked up, her oval face pale and shadowy around the eyes. "Please just say whatever you came to say and then go, Mr. Farrell." She didn't know if she could stand much more of this. Just looking at him was making her stomach churn, remembering. The sound of his voice was different. It had been warm and light-hearted that night. But it would always make her body jerk with pain whenever she heard it because she was never going to forget that night.

"I just had a visitor," he said, watching her. "He said his name was Porter."

"Oh!" Natasha burst out, whitening and aghast as realization dawned on her. How had Mike found out? Nigel, she thought. Nigel had told him. Of course. Why hadn't it occurred to her that he would? She had been so busy worrying about Nigel's reaction to the news that she was pregnant that she hadn't even gone on to imagine that he would at once tell Mike about Lee Farrell.

Lee Farrell's mouth twisted. "I see we begin to talk the same language," he said.

Her cheeks began to burn as her color came back in a heated flood. He knew about the baby. She couldn't meet his eyes. She was so embarrassed she could have sunk through the floor. She turned and walked across the room to get away from the biting scrutiny of those icy gray eyes, and he followed her.

"I was asleep in bed. I've just got back from the States and I went to bed suffering from jet lag. I didn't hear the doorbell. The first I knew was when I realized someone was trying to kick my front door down."

She winced. *Oh, Mike, how could you,* she thought miserably. It was so pointless.

"When I finally struggled downstairs and opened the door someone came through it like a charging bull. I was still groggy or he'd never have got away with it, but before I had time to realize what was happening he had knocked me flat on my back.''

She sat down suddenly in the nearest chair, her hands over her hot face.

Lee Farrell's voice had the raw sting of a winter wind in it. "He called me a string of charming names without bothering to explain who he was or what was going on," he told her. "I thought he was some raving lunatic with a grudge. I've met those before.''

"I'm sorry," Natasha whispered.

"I'm sure you are," he flung back tersely.

"I didn't tell him," she said, lifting her head, her hands dropping from her face and her blue eyes, bright with unshed tears, staring at him.

"What sort of fool do you take me for?" he snarled.

"I didn't!''

"Don't tell me—he has a crystal ball!''

"Nigel told him," she muttered, bending her head on a weary movement, her long black hair flowing down against her flushed skin and tumbling over her shoulders.

His brows met. "Nigel?" There was a brief silence, then he said, "The guy you were with? The idiot with the sports car?''

She nodded.

She heard him move restlessly. He walked across the room and back again in an impatient way. She didn't look up but she could sense the hesitation, the anger, the doubt inside him from the way he walked, his long legs striding forward and checking with irritation as he met the wall, the swing of his body as he turned back filled with controlled fury.

"Look, I don't know who told him, but he wouldn't have tried to blackmail me if—''

"Blackmail you?" Natasha's head flew up again, her mouth open in disbelief.

Lee Farrell halted and stood in front of her, his eyes searching her face. "Yes, ugly word, isn't it?" He smiled grimly. "An ugly business all around."

"What do you mean, blackmail you?" she asked, stammering the words out. "What are you talking about?"

"My God, will you drop the pretense of amazed innocence?" he erupted, flashing a caustic look at her. "What the hell is the point? We both know what I'm talking about. You sent Porter around to see me—"

"No!"

His lips curled back from bared white teeth. "Yes," he insisted. "He wasn't acting on his own. You sent him. I'll give you this—you're the best actress I've ever met and you must be as smart as a whip, too. I didn't think I'd ever get caught in a trap like this but there's always the first time, and I'll admit I'm well and truly caught. I've no doubt you planned it together—you'll have thought of all the angles. But we'll play it by the book, all the same. I'll want blood tests before I part with one shilling."

"Blood tests?" she faltered, staring at him.

"I want proof that it's mine." His mouth twisted nastily. "Although I'm sure it is. You're too clever to risk fostering someone else's baby on me. I'll pay, but first I want proof positive that it is mine."

Natasha struggled to her feet, a hammer pounding at her forehead. "I don't want you to—"

He didn't let her finish. "What you want, lady, is of absolutely no consequence to me. From now on, I call the tune, since it appears I'm going to have to pay the piper. When it is born you'll hand it over to me and you'll never come near me or the baby again—"

"Listen to me," Natasha burst out, interrupting him. She felt she was going crazy. Everything he had said was so inexplicable. Mike had asked him for money? Blackmailed him? She couldn't believe it. It wasn't possible. Mike was not that sort of man. There must be some mistake. Lee Farrell must have misunderstood Mike.

"I've listened to Porter," Lee Farrell said curtly. "That was enough, thank you. At least he was direct. He just came out with it. He didn't pretend it was anything other than a blunt demand for money. And if it is mine, I'll pay. It will have been a very expensive night's entertainment, but I'd rather pay through the nose than think of a child of mine growing up with a two-faced little bitch like you."

She backed in pale dismay from the harsh expression on his face as he spat that at her.

"We'll do it legally this time," he went on. "You'll get your money once I know for certain that the child is mine. I'll get my lawyers to draw up a contract. You'll sign it before I hand over the money and if you ever try to see either me or the child again, you'll find yourself in serious trouble, I promise you. I'll make sure the contract is watertight." He gave her one long, sweeping hostile look, then turned and walked to the door while she stood frozen in dumb incredulity.

The slam of the door made her start forward. She was shaking as she ran after him. He was taking the stairs two at a time and he did not halt or look back when she urgently called his name.

She ran down the stairs after him, but when she got to the street she was just in time to see Mike get out of his car, turn and halt as Lee Farrell strode past him. Natasha's nerves jumped as Lee Farrell stopped in his tracks. The two men looked at each other in naked hostility, bristling visibly. Natasha had the feeling they were about to go for each other's throats. They seemed poised for violence, bodies tense, faces angry. She stumbled forward, a strangled plea whispering from her. She didn't even know what she was saying. The words came out without Natasha being aware of them. Lee Farrell glanced over his shoulder briefly, his eyes scathing, then he turned and walked to his car, got into it and shot away, tires screeching.

Mike looked at Natasha bitterly. "So he's been here. I might have known. What was he doing? Trying to buy his way out of it?"

His voice was too loud. The street was quiet. She felt every ear in every house tuned to what Mike was shouting at her.

"Come in," she muttered, going back to the house.

He followed her. They went upstairs in silence, but as they took the final stairs she heard her neighbor's door open a crack. She pretended not to notice. No doubt the nurse was dying of curiosity, which wasn't surprising after all the noisy comings and goings.

Mike banged the door behind him. It seemed necessary to relieve the anger in him. Natasha looked at him miserably.

"Why did you go and see him? How could you, Mike?"

"Why?" he threw back at her. "The bastard had my girl. I wanted to smash his face through the back of his head."

Natasha flinched from that tone. "You had no right."

"No right? No bloody right? We were going to get married," Mike said harshly, looking at her as if he had never seen her before.

"You broke off the engagement," she reminded him.

He gave a thick groan. "Oh, Natasha...." He turned and walked to the wall and leaned his head on it like an unhappy child. She watched him for a moment, wanting to cry, then she went over and put a tentative hand on his shoulder.

"Mike, don't. I'm sorry."

"Have you any idea how I feel? How could you do a thing like that?" He had his face turned away from her but she felt the muscles in his shoulder knotted with tension. "You've never let me get anywhere near taking you to bed and I accepted that you wanted to wait, then you go off and sleep with a total stranger? How could you?"

"You don't think I planned it? I drank too much. I'd never have behaved like that otherwise."

She felt the shudder he gave. "It was him," he muttered incoherently. "That bastard. Herries told me he picked you up, he told me all about it. Farrell's got a track record. He goes through women at a rate of knots, according to Herries. If he sees one he fancies he just walks off with her."

Natasha felt sick. No doubt he did. She wasn't surprised to hear that, remembering the cool way he had whisked her away from Nigel.

"I was sure it was Herries. I was all set to beat him into a cinder, then he told me it was Farrell and where I could find him."

Natasha listened with shame and miserable anxiety. How would she ever be able to face Nigel Herries again? The very idea made her skin crawl. The thought of Mike shouting accusations at him, Nigel's surprise and curiosity, his dawning amusement, made her ill.

"He told me Farrell was one of these jet-set cowboys, with money to burn and women lined up in queues, and when I got to Farrell's place I saw Herries hadn't exaggerated. The house was furnished like a palace, and while I was talking to Farrell a woman came to the top of the stairs. She was a sexy redhead and she wasn't wearing a stitch under her negligee. I could see right through it. She knew and she didn't care. She gave me a long look and walked into his bedroom." Mike turned haggard eyes on Natasha. "Oh, you certainly picked a lovely guy to take your revenge with."

"I wasn't," she began, and he glared at her.

"Yes, that was exactly what you were doing. You were sticking a knife into me because I wouldn't walk out on my mother."

"You're wrong, Mike! None of it happened deliberately. I got drunk."

He sneered and she felt anger shoot through the top of her head. "And, anyway, what has it got to do with you anymore? We're not engaged. You broke it off. You blamed me because your mother can't stand the sight of me. She can't stand Kenneth's wife, either, can she? She can't stand the idea of any woman coming between her and her sons. Your mother wants both of you all to herself." She stopped the angry flood of words as she caught sight of Mike's pale, stunned face.

His breath came roughly. "That's a lie."

"Is it? Have you ever talked to Kenneth about it?"

she asked him in a gentler tone, her face anxious because she saw that she had distressed him.

"You've never even met my brother! What makes you think you know more about him than I do?"

"I've heard your mother talking about him and his wife. That was enough. She wasn't going to give me a chance, Mike. It might have worked for us if you hadn't tried to insist that we live with her, but you wouldn't listen to me and now it is all too late."

He looked at her miserably. "Natasha, why did you do it?" The anger had drained out of his face and there was hopelessness in his voice. She knew the feeling. It was how she felt herself.

"I told you. I was unhappy and I went a little crazy."

He sighed, nodding. "And you had to meet that bastard. I wish I'd done more than knock him down. I wish I'd broken his neck."

Natasha looked at him hesitantly. "He said you asked him for money."

"What?" Mike looked blankly at her, his brown eyes puzzled.

"He claimed you tried to blackmail him."

Mike flushed and bristled with aggression. "That's a damned lie. Blackmail him? Why—" He broke off, forehead wrinkled. "I told him he was going to pay," he said slowly. "That was all I said. But I wasn't talking about money. I never mentioned money."

"I thought it must be something like that," Natasha murmured, feeling relieved. She had known that Mike wouldn't do anything of the sort, but Lee Farrell had been so certain and Natasha had been too off balance to be able to trust to her own instincts about people.

Mike was staring at her, frowning. "What did he say? Is that why he was here?"

She nodded. "He thought you and I were trying to blackmail him."

"I'll kill him," Mike hissed through his teeth, his fists clenching. "I'll break every bone in his body."

"No," she said. "Stay away from him, Mike." Enough damage had been done. She had had enough. She took a long painful breath. "Stay away from me, too, from now on."

His head lifted and he looked at her, his eyes filling with pain. "Natasha." He took a step toward her and she retreated, her hand lifted in mute denial. She shook her head. "I mean it," she told him.

He stopped and stood there, staring at her.

"Everything's loused up," Natasha said huskily. "We might as well face it. It's over."

He moved restlessly, his face full of conflicting feelings. She could read them all. She knew Mike still cared for her, just as she still cared for him, but they were two people on the opposite sides of a great gulf and she knew they were never going to bridge the empty space between them. Mike knew it, too. He knew it was over.

"What will you do?" he asked. "How will you manage?"

"Somehow," Natasha said.

"If you need any help—"

She shook her head, smiling too brightly. "No, it's kind of you, but no."

He shifted his feet, looking down. "It's Farrell's problem, too," he muttered.

"No, it isn't. It's mine and only mine and I don't

want him brought into it." Her voice was firm and determined.

"You haven't thought about it, Natasha!"

"I've thought of nothing else for the last day or so."

"It will be very tough for you."

"I'll manage."

"Will you go home?"

She hesitated, about to say no, then said, "Maybe."

Mike looked relieved, which was what she had wanted. "That would be the best solution. Your family can help you. It won't be easy looking after a baby on your own."

"No." She wanted him to go. It hurt to have him standing there. Only a short time ago they had been so happy and looking forward to a future together that was to have been one long, glorious honeymoon. Now their future was ashes and she could only look forward to a grim struggle to cope with the life of an unmarried mother.

Mike had the look of a man who wanted to go yet couldn't bring himself to say goodbye. She glanced at him wryly.

"You'd better go, Mike."

He still didn't move, torn between conflicting emotions. "Natasha, I—"

"Please," she broke in. "Please, just go. There's nothing more to be said."

He closed his eyes and nodded, then came over and kissed her on the cheek. "God bless."

Only when he had gone did she start to cry.

CHAPTER FIVE

SHE WAS LISTENING TO THE RADIO that evening when someone knocked at the door. Warily, Natasha opened it and felt color stain her cheeks as she looked into Nigel's face.

He caught hold of the edge of the door as though he suspected she might slam it in his face. "I want to talk to you."

She could imagine what about. She couldn't hold his eyes. "Please go away, Nigel," she said in a voice thick with embarrassment and distress.

"Won't you just listen?" He pushed the door open a little wider and she fell back. Nigel walked into the room and looked around it while Natasha slowly shut the door.

"You know Mike Porter came to see me?" he asked.

"Yes." She knew. Why was he here? Had he come to pry and probe and find out some more fascinating details of what had happened? She had never liked him much, but she felt she hated him at this moment. It wasn't pleasant to know that someone regarded you as some sort of sideshow at a fairground. It make her sick to realize that Nigel knew what had happened between her and Lee Farrell, and even more sick to know he was bound to pass on the scandal embellished with every frill he could find out or invent.

"Bad luck," he said, and he sounded quite serious. She was surprised into looking at him and there was none of the glee she had expected to see in his face. He was frowning, staring at her with curiosity, but not with malice. "I don't suppose you want to talk, but I just wanted to say that so far as I'm concerned it makes no difference."

Natasha stared at him.

"Where you job's concerned," he added, seeing her blank face. "I mean, well, these things happen. We all make mistakes. I thought you might be worried and I don't want to lose you. You're a good secretary. Until— well, until you have to stop work, I hope you'll carry on as normal."

Natasha realized with a shock that Nigel was embarrassed. He was faintly pink and his voice was rough.

"Thank you," she said slowly.

"It must have been a terrific shock for you."

She nodded, looking away.

"I won't hang around," Nigel said, turning back toward the door. "Just came to say that. Thought you might be at your wit's end. You're not the type to handle this sort of trouble without—" He broke off. "Anyway, don't worry. Nobody's going to make moral noises at you at the firm, you know. We're all broadminded. It could have happened to any of us."

People are unpredictable, Natasha thought as he went out. She had misjudged Nigel. His offer certainly took the immediate pressure off her. She followed him to the door and he stopped and looked at her hesitantly. "I won't tell anyone," he said, and somehow she believed him. "When I was eighteen my girl friend thought she was pregnant," he muttered. "Luckily it was a false alarm. Horrible moment, though, for both of us. She was still at school. Her parents would have killed me.''

When he had walked away down the stairs Natasha closed the door, half smiling. So that explained his odd sympathy. Fellow feeling. For once she had struck a genuine vein in Nigel Herries. She had reminded him of a real emotion he had once felt himself. People's motives were so tangled and so self-obsessed and hard to read.

All the same, she had a much lighter heart as she got ready for bed. At least she would not have to start looking for a new job, nor, if Nigel kept his word, would she have to go into work the next day knowing that everyone was staring at her curiously or laughing behind her back. Life would be much easier if you lived on a desert island where there was no one to complicate things, she thought. Apart from the financial problems that her situation was going to bring, a good deal of her anxiety and shock had been due to the horrible public embarrassment she had known she was going to face. It would have taken enormous courage to walk into the office next morning if she had been expecting everyone to know about what had happened.

Even now she wasn't quite sure what she was going to face. When she arrived at the office she was stiff with tension, her smile brittle when she crossed from the lift to her office.

Nigel arrived late and had a client closeted with him all morning. Natasha found it hard at first to meet his eyes, but as the day wore on it got much easier. They were very busy, which helped. Nigel was in one of his active phases. The ebb and flow of his temperament meant that he worked in fits and starts, and today he was having a creative jag. Ideas were leaping from him like salmon from a river. Gradually Natasha found herself forgetting her own problems as she got more and more involved in work. Nigel didn't say a syllable about her private life. He was totally absorbed in himself again, which made him very cheerful, particularly when one of the graphics team came into the office to show him something. It wasn't the artwork he liked. It was the girl's streamlined, slinky body and the inviting way she smiled at him as they glanced through the sketches together.

By the time the girl left Nigel had fixed up a date with her. "To discuss this project," he explained and the girl gave him a mocking smile.

"Of course," she said as she left.

Nigel whistled happily, brushing back his floppy hair, and Natasha briefly envied him that ability to be self-absorbed. Nigel was a hedonist; loving pleasure and only interested in himself, and he took life lightly, which was just fine for Nigel. He kept her working late that afternoon because he wanted to get down that stream of ideas on paper before he forgot them, and Natasha was quite cheerful about staying. She owed Nigel a favor. He had been decent about her problem and he had given her a slightly different view of him. He might have personal reasons for being sympathetic over her situation, but it was still decent of him and she was grateful. She knew she would never feel the same dislike of him again.

Her bus crawled jerkily through the congested traffic as she made her way home. London was crowded, the pavements full of jostling pedestrians, the roads full of cars and taxis. Natasha stared out of the window at the sea of anonymous faces and felt as though she were a visitor from another time and place, looking into a living world in which she had no part, in which she did not belong. There was more than glass between herself and all those busy hurrying people. She was an accident victim who was walking about with fatal injuries unnoticed. She struggled with the reality that she carried within her, trying to come to terms with the inescapable nature of her situation. At this moment there was no outward sign to alert anyone who saw her. She looked perfectly normal. One tiny, hidden part of her body was changed, though. The life within her was still merely a developing seed, yet its presence had changed her whole future, just as much as if she had walked out into this busy road and been knocked down by a car.

It was the chance nature of that collision with fate that made her feel bitterly resentful. When she looked back to the morning in the park when she and Mike quarreled she heard a string of ifs. If she had been more tactful, if Mike had been less blinkered, if she hadn't been so reckless in accepting Nigel's invitation to that party, if she hadn't got drunk and gone off with Lee Farrell. If, if, if.

There was only pointless futility in quarreling with fate. Fate in this case was only another name for her own folly. It had all happened. She bore the consequence inside her. There was nothing she could do but accept it.

She wasn't hungry but it kept her occupied to get herself some supper. She had some salad and some cheese and was just washing up when there was a knock at the door. Natasha hesitated, half inclined to pretend she wasn't at home. The knock came louder and then she heard the nurse's voice outside and walked to open the door, dragging a polite smile across her face.

It had not been the nurse who had knocked, though. She was on the landing, talking in a lively, hopeful way to Lee Farrell, and her presence meant that Natasha had to somehow hold that smile.

The nurse jammed her small navy-blue cap on to her head. "I'm just off," she said to Natasha regretfully. "Night duty."

"Oh, too bad," Natasha said with an effort that cost her a good deal. "Don't work too hard."

"Lucky if I have the choice," said the other girl, laughing loudly. Lee Farrell calmly walked past Natasha, who had no option but to allow it. The nurse looked after him and sighed heavily. She gave Natasha a wink. "Lucky girl," she whispered. "I wouldn't mind finding him in my stocking next Christmas."

Natasha pretended to laugh. The nurse walked off and Natasha closed the door, turning to look at Lee Farrell. He was standing in the middle of the room, his head bent as if the cap of his shoe fascinated him.

"Mr. Farrell, I was going to write to you tonight. You got it all wrong—"

"I know," he said tersely.

Natasha stiffened, her lips parted in surprise. "You know?"

"Porter came to see me again." He looked up, his face pale. "That's why I'm here. To say I'm sorry."

"Oh," she said, some of the bitter tension draining

out of her. She had keyed herself up to explain to him how mistaken he had been, and it was a relief to find it had been done for her.

"I must have entirely misunderstood him. He was in a temper and talking wildly. I leaped to the wrong conclusions."

"Yes."

"I said some rotten things to you." He looked at her restlessly, then away, little red spots in his cheeks, his black lashes flickering against his skin.

"You were upset," Natasha said, and he laughed harshly.

"An understatement." He shot her another look. "I'm a very wealthy man; I'm what some people see as an easy target. When Porter started threatening me, saying I was going to pay through the nose, I got the wrong impression."

"I do understand," she said, wanting only to have him go away. "There's no need to say any more."

"No need on your side, maybe," he muttered. "On mine, there is. I feel pretty foul about what I said to you, the way I treated you, especially when you're already very upset and worried."

"It doesn't matter. Forget it." That was all she wanted to do—forget the misery she had felt yesterday and that she was likely to feel again tomorrow. She had an endless procession of tomorrows to face and she did not know how she was going to get through them, but she did know that she did not want Lee Farrell in her flat, in her life, reminding her, complicating things that were already overcomplicated.

"Forget it?" He drew an unsteady breath and looked at her violently, his gray eyes obsidian. "Are you serious? How the hell am I supposed to forget that you're carrying my child?''

Her color flowed hotly and her blue eyes dropped to the middle button of his dark waistcoat. ''If you're ready to listen to me this time, Mr. Farrell, I'd like to make it quite clear that I don't want anything from you. I'll deal with it without help. It's my problem, not yours.''

''It's my baby!''

''No,'' Natasha said, still staring at that button, her face burning. ''It is mine,''

He moved impatiently. ''All right, let me rephrase that. It is ours, we've both involved, just as we both—''

''Don't,'' she interrupted, biting her lower lip until it hurt. ''You don't understand. I just want you to go away and forget you ever met me.''

''Don't be bloody ridiculous,'' he erupted, the masculine violence making her jump as though she had opened a furnace door and felt the savage heat flaming out at her.

Her flinching did not go unnoticed. He watched her, breathing fiercely, then he moved closer and she kept her eyes lowered, her face stiff and nervous.

Gently he said, ''Be realistic. You need help and I'm the obvious person to help you. You can't go through this alone. You haven't thought about it.''

''I've thought about nothing else,'' she said, laughing bitterly.

He put a hand on her flowing dark hair softly and she drew back in an involuntary movement of rejection. His hand fell away and he stiffened.

''You know the obvious solution,'' he said flatly. ''You must marry me.''

Natasha looked up, her face startled. "Marry you?" She had not expected that. Her lips were parted on an intake of incredulous breath, then she shook her head fiercely. "Of course I won't marry you. That would be worse, can't you see that?"

"Worse?" He seemed taken aback.

"Worse than having the baby by myself. I'd be saddled with a husband I don't want, too." She was too distraught to choose her words carefully, and she saw the red color invade his face, caught the flash of the gray eyes. She had insulted him and he was very angry.

Before he could retort, she hurriedly said, "I'm sorry, I could have put that better."

"You could."

"But I was being honest. I don't want this baby, but neither do I want—"

"Me?" he interrupted icily, his brows a black line across his forehead, and Natasha sighed.

"To marry a reluctant husband," she corrected quietly. "You don't want to marry me any more than I want to marry you. Why on earth should you? We've only met twice. We barely know each other."

"I'd say we knew each other intimately," he said with an oddly twisted little smile, and she felt sick as she met his eyes.

"You know what I mean," she said with hostility. "What sort of marriage would we have? Use your head, Mr. Farrell. It would be a disaster. It wouldn't work. We'd both resent the situation. Is that any way to bring up a child?"

He studied her in silence for a moment. "Face the alternatives," he said after a while. "If you don't marry me how are you going to cope?"

"I will keep on my job while I can. I haven't explored the possibilities any further than that yet, but I will. I've no doubt I'll find a way. There's always a way if you look for it."

He walked to a chair and sat down, leaning back with his arms crossed behind the back of his head. Lamplight gave his black hair a glossy sheen. The gray eyes were thoughtful.

"Sit down," he ordered, and she bristled.

"Mr. Farrell—"

"Sit down." The tone cracked like a whip, and Natasha found herself resentfully obeying. It was a relief, she realized. Her legs were weak. The moment she sat down she felt aware of her own shaky state of nerves. She laced her fingers in her lap to hide the way they were trembling.

"How old are you?" he asked.

"What's that to do—"

"How old?" he insisted.

"Twenty-two," she said, then met his eyes and added reluctantly, "Nearly."

His mouth was crooked. "So you're twenty-one?"

She nodded, resentment in her face. "But I'm quite capable of looking after myself and I don't need your help."

"I've seen how good you are at looking after yourself," he told her dryly.

"That was different. I was crazy that night."

"You were unhappy and you did something reckless," he said, and she nodded. "That could be a dangerous pattern," Lee Farrell said quietly.

"It won't be a pattern. I won't make that mistake again. I'm not really the reckless type."

"You're the emotional type," he said, his eyes unreadable. "Very female."

"You make that sound like an accusation."

"Just a statement of fact. You react like a woman. Women tend to act first and think afterward, and that can be disastrous."

"That's a sexist remark," Natasha muttered. "I'm perfectly rational most of the time, and I resent being told I'm incapable of thinking straight because I'm a woman."

"You aren't thinking straight if you imagine that a girl of your age is going to be able to bring up a baby without any help. In any case, whether you like it or not, the fact remains—it's my baby, too."

Natasha shifted uneasily. "Only by accident, it could have been—" She broke off, meeting his eyes, and saw his mouth tighten.

"You have a genius for using words like blunt instruments," he said angrily. "It could have been any man, that's what you were going to say, wasn't it?"

Very flushed, she didn't answer.

"But it wasn't any man," he said through tight lips. "It was me, however you feel about that now, and I insist on my right as the father to look after this child. We'll leave you out of it, as you seem to find it so distasteful to admit I'm involved. Just get it through your head that this is my baby, too, and I want to take my share of the responsibility for it."

Tears glazed her blue eyes as she looked up at him again. "I didn't intend to be hurtful. Can't you see how I feel?"

"Very clearly," he told her in a curt voice. "You were in love with Porter."

"I still am," she said on a strangled sob, and bent her head to cover the surge of pain that had forced its way through. She struggled with tears for a moment, biting her lip, trembling.

Lee Farrell moved. He sat on the arm of her chair, thrust an arm around her and pulled her against his chest in a rough movement that she couldn't fight against. Natasha found her face pressed into his waistcoat, the hard rim of a button forced into her cheek. He soothingly stroked her hair in a way that was not sexually intrusive. The comforting fingers took on a rhythm that quietened her.

"Porter can't forgive you?" he asked above her head. She sighed, not answering.

"He struck me as a rather aggressive young man of limited sympathy," he said, half to himself.

"That's not fair," Natasha broke out, moving away from him and then regretting it because she was finding the soothing movements of his hands so comforting. She looked at him. "It has been a shock for him, too. It's all such a mess."

"If he loved you he would realize it was partly his fault."

"That wouldn't alter the fact that I'm expecting somebody else's child," Natasha said miserably. "And if his mother ever found out she would never let me forget it, either of us forget it. Even if Mike asked me I wouldn't marry him now."

Lee Farrell studied her curiously. "You're an obstinate little creature, aren't you? But you have your own weird sort of integrity."

She half smiled. "Thank you."

He took out a handkerchief and dried her face delicately, a finger under her chin to tilt it his way. Still holding it, he looked into her raised eyes. "I'm going to open a bank account for you."

"No," she said, and he put a finger on her lips to silence her.

"I'll give you a straight choice. Either you marry me now or you accept a legal arrangement. I can always take you to court, you know."

She was staggered, her eyes huge. "To court? Don't be absurd. For what? What do you mean, take me to court?"

"You're not the type to lie in the witness box," Lee Farrell said mockingly. "If I get you into court you'll have to admit I'm the father of the baby, and the court will give me the right to have some say in the way it is brought up."

Natasha eyed him. "That sounds like blackmail."

"Don't force me to use it," he advised. "Accept the money. You needn't use it until the time comes. All I want to do is minimize the worries you're going to have and share some of the burden with you."

"You're being very kind," she said, her lips trembling into a weak smile.

He watched her mouth, his face blank. "You agree?"

She nodded reluctantly. "I appreciate the offer." There was a troubled little silence between them as though the long tug of war had made them both mentally exhausted, and now neither knew quite what to say. Natasha asked politely, "Can I get you some coffee?"

"Please," he said, and she got up and went over to the little electric stove on which she cooked. He watched her and then glanced around the room, his face wry.

"You won't be able to stay here for long, you know. Once the landlord realizes—"

"Yes," she said, cutting him short. That had occurred to her.

"I'll find somewhere better," Lee Farrell said, and Natasha bristled crossly.

"You will not! Stop trying to run my life for me. I'll find a place myself when the time comes."

He held up a hand. "All right, all right. Don't get into another state. What about your family? Told them yet?"

She shook her head. The kettle boiled. She made instant coffee in two mugs while he watched her. Carrying it back toward him she said, "I'll have to sometime but—"

"You can't face it yet?"

She shook her head again. "They are going to be so hurt."

He took one of the mugs and held it in both hands, looking at her as she sat down in the other chair. "Wouldn't it be easier all round if you married me, Natasha?" he asked gently. "You wouldn't have any problems at all, then."

"Wrong," Natasha said shakily. "I'd just have a different set of problems, that's all."

He stared down into the coffee. "So you prefer to struggle on alone and face it all rather than face marriage to me?"

He put it rather strangely, but she nodded. "If I can get over the next couple of years I may be okay," she said, searching for a way of making him understand how she felt. "But if I marry you I'd have a problem for life."

His mouth was hard and tight. "I'm obviously as desirable as foot-and-mouth disease," he said, and Natasha laughed in faint hysteria.

"I'm sorry. I didn't mean—"

"Don't expand on what you've already said," he pleaded coolly. "I don't think I could stand it. If I ever saw myself as the answer to a maiden's prayer, you've disillusioned me today."

CHAPTER SIX

SEVERAL DAYS LATER she was filing in her office, a pile of folders at her elbow, when Sonia Warren sauntered into the room on a cloud of expensive perfume and gave a catlike smile. "Nigel in?"

Natasha shook her head, picking up another file and slotting it into the filing cabinet. Out of the corner of her eye she saw Sonia take a seat on the edge of the desk, one long silk-clad leg swinging and her body in an elegant pose. The green dress she wore had a plunging neckline that advertised her femininity without pretense and the hitch of her skirt as she lounged there watching Natasha exposed most of her legs. A pity Nigel wasn't around to enjoy it, Natasha thought grimly, slamming the cabinet shut.

"Can I help you?" she asked politely, turning around.

"Not really. I want to talk to Nigel."

"He should be back in an hour. Can I get him to call you?"

"Yes, do that." Sonia leaned back, both hands gripping the desk, presenting her ultrafeminine figure like a carefully carved sculpture, her head flung back. Natasha had seen her do it a hundred times. Sonia was always very conscious of her sexy figure. Usually Sonia ignored her, but today there was a malicious glint in her eyes.

"See Lee Farrell lately?"

Natasha felt color steal into her cheeks at the question and was angry with herself for betraying so much. Sonia's eyes narrowed watchfully.

"Not lately," Natasha said. Not for a couple of days, anyway, she told herself, so it wasn't so much a lie as a conscious evasion.

"Lost interest, did he?" The malice came out into the open with that question. Sonia ran a spiteful stare down Natasha's figure. "I wouldn't have said you were his type. He usually likes them rather more obvious." She gave Natasha a pretense of a smile. "Not that I'm knocking you, darling."

"No, of course not," Natasha said, looking at her with dislike.

"But let's face it, you're hardly the type to knock them down in the street. You're the quiet type."

"Mousy?" Natasha suggested tartly.

Sonia smiled, all honey. "No, darling, I didn't mean that. Don't put words in my mouth. You're...an acquired taste," she said, giving Natasha another lingering inspection, her mouth curving in smiling dismissal, which told Natasha as clearly as words could have done that Sonia could not imagine who, if anybody, was ever likely to acquire a taste so boring.

"Lee's spoiled for choice, of course," Sonia purred. "His job gives him so much variety to choose from."

Natasha realized in surprise that she had no idea what job Lee Farrell did. It had never come up in conversation.

"What is his job?" she asked involuntarily, and Sonia gave her a quick, shrewd look.

"You don't know?"

"He didn't mention it."

She got another sweet-sour smile from Sonia. "Too busy in another direction, was he?"

The trouble with that little dig was that it was unfortunately all too close to the truth, and Natasha looked away.

"He manages Starlight Records. They were quite small five years ago, but they've been expanding fast."

"I've never heard of them," Natasha said, but then she knew nothing of the music world and only the names of the giant record companies meant anything to her.

"They put out Lara Brennan's discs," Sonia said, watching her with an odd expression.

Natasha had heard of Lara Brennan. "She just got into the top ten with that song about a fairground, didn't she? I heard it a few times on the radio."

Sonia had a smile on her face, the sort of smile a cat wears as it pounces on a mouse. "She's also Lee Farrell's latest mistress." The words came out as slick as a knife, and Sonia watched Natasha to see how they sunk in.

Natasha couldn't control the faint quiver of shock passing over her face. Her lashes flickered rapidly as she looked down.

"Oh?" she said with an effort.

"Now she *is* Lee's type," Sonia said. "*Very* obvious, that lady. Bedroom eyes and a figure to go with them. No prizes for guessing what he sees in her."

The phone rang and Natasha picked it up. Sonia slid down off the desk and wandered away to the door. She gave Natasha a brief glance over one shoulder. "See you, darling. Get Nigel to give me a ring, won't you?"

Natasha nodded, speaking into the telephone. It was the art department, and she was kept talking for five minutes. When she put the phone down she stared out of the window. So, she thought, Lee Farrell was having an affair with one of the singers who worked for his company. So what? His behavior the night she met him had given her a clear indication of his sexual standards. He had walked off with her and taken her to bed without a second's hesitation. She would have been crazy if she had imagined there was anything new in that as far as he was concerned. Standard procedure, no doubt. He did it all the time. She had realized afterward that it had meant nothing to him. A one-night stand, she thought, wincing. Not a nice label to stick on oneself. But that was how he saw her, of course.

Why did she feel that stupid niggle of pain? She wasn't in love with him. She liked him. That was all. It was rather absurd to feel shaken by the news that he had other women. What on earth had she expected? She had gone to bed with him on impulse and she hadn't meant to see him again when she got back to normal the next day. Wasn't she imposing a double standard when she felt angry with him now?

Nigel breezed into the office an hour later, looking pleased with himself. He had just snatched a contract away from some rivals and was cock-a-hoop over it. He burst into self-praise, beaming, then broke off giving Natasha a shrewd look. "You're very lackluster. Feeling low? I've got just the cure for that."

She stiffened, her eyes freezing over and he held up one hand. "Wait for it, wait for it. Don't jump down my throat before I've said anything to get nasty about. I was going to say that I'm going to see that new play at the Apollo theater with some friends tonight. There's a ticket going spare. Want to come?"

"That's very kind," Natasha said, hesitation in her voice.

"It's supposed to be good," Nigel told her. "There'll be six of us—plenty of protection for you." His smile was faintly piqued and sulky. "I just thought it would take you out of yourself."

"Thank you, I'd love to," she said, feeling rather ashamed of having jumped to the wrong conclusions. Nigel wasn't as black as she had always painted him, but it was difficult to remember that. Her instincts always prompted her to run when he asked her out anywhere.

"Fine," he said. "We planned to have supper afterward. There won't be time for more than a drink before the curtain."

She nodded, smiling a little shyly at him.

"By the way, Sonia Warren dropped in and asked if you would ring her," she told him, and he looked interested.

"I wonder what she wants?" He moved to the door of his own office. "Get her on the line for me, will you?"

She dialed Sonia's number. The feline voice purred, "Sonia Warren speaking."

"Natasha here. I've got Nigel for you, Sonia."

Sonia laughed, a sound like tinkling ice. "Darling, I've had him and it didn't set the Thames on fire."

Natasha refused to play that game of verbal innuendo. Gritting her teeth she switched Sonia through and put down her own receiver. Sometimes she wished she worked for some nice quiet firm, an accountant's office or a solicitor's, where women like Sonia Warren and men like Nigel did not play elaborate and meaningless games that had a thread of malice and self-indulgence running through them. The advertising business leaned heavily on sex to sell their products. The whole atmosphere reeked of it. Artwork gave the visual signals—sleek young bodies in brief clothes or none at all. The copy followed through with the same subliminal suggestion—get the right brand of sex and you get the best life has to offer, from a limousine to a mink coat or the best brand of butter. Whatever you had to sell to the public, sex could sell. Natasha had often felt like a salmon swimming upriver in that office, faced with a consensus of opinion she could not agree with, reluctant to get involved in arguments that would mean she was branded naive or gauche because her personal, private views were different than those around her.

Ironic, she thought, looking dully out of the window. She would never have imagined herself going to bed with a strange man, and she had certainly not imagined herself pregnant in these circumstances.

Perhaps the subliminal suggestions had been working away inside her head without her realizing it. When she was faced with a painful personal problem she had followed the advice handed out in this office for any problem. "Sex always works." It always worked its magic. It always sold the product. *But not for me,* Natasha thought grimly. Oh, no, never again. The morality her parents had drummed into her head had had reinforcement of a bitter kind. She wouldn't forget it.

The play that evening was light and lively. The audience loved it. So did Nigel and his friends. Natasha wanted to like it. She wanted to laugh and relax and let the bright bubbles of words float around her. But she couldn't. She was, Nigel said severely, "Very uptight, darling. Like an elastic band that's pulled too tight. You'll snap."

"Sorry," she said, smiling as brightly as she could.

He half slapped, half patted her hand. "Naughty; we wanted to cheer you up."

"A drink would do it," one of the others said, winking at Natasha.

"Good thinking," Nigel congratulated him, pulling Natasha out of her seat. "Come on."

The bar was crowded. Natasha stood in the circle of people, a glass in her hand, pretending to listen and wishing she was back in her quiet flat alone. She could not rid herself of this strange feeling of being apart, an outsider, as though she carried some invisible brand that marked her.

"You're not drinking!" Nigel complained, looking at her barely touched glass.

"I'm okay," she said, because she was not going to repeat her folly at that party. Never again was she going to use drink as a crutch. She had done so once and had been left crippled for life.

It was as they were going back to their seats that she saw Lee Farrell. He was down in the stalls. Nigel had got seats in the circle and as she walked down the steps to their row Natasha stared at Lee Farrell's black head absently. She hadn't noticed him earlier. He was sitting beside a redheaded girl in a cool coffee-colored dress. She was laughing, her head turned toward him. Natasha distinctly saw her put a hand on his leg and her nerves jumped in shock. She looked away, frowning. It was absurd to feel that jag of hurt because another woman touched him. He wasn't her property. Far from it. She had sent him away firmly because there was nothing between them but the memory of a few crazy hours.

She settled in her seat, bending her head over the program, and resolutely did not look their way again.

After the final curtain call they all made their way out of the theater into the confused muddle on the pavement. "Supper," Nigel reminded her. "We've booked a table."

"Oh, I don't—" Natasha began, and he crossly took her hand and shook it as though she were a six-year-old.

"Don't argue. Nigel knows best."

Someone behind them said in a deep, cold voice, "Excuse me."

Nigel moved aside to let two people pass, glanced at them, then did a double take, recognizing Lee Farrell.

Natasha had recognized the voice at once. Her mind had jerked with shock. Lee's voice had been so icy, so remote. She had looked at him involuntarily then hurriedly looked away. The imprint of his image remained in her mind, the long lean body giving off a potent sexuality as he shouldered his way through the crowd, his dark suit and smoothly shaven face very formal and elegant.

Although she hadn't been looking at her, Natasha had caught sight of the redhead with him. She had been clutching his dark sleeve and tottering beside him on very high heels, her curved body wrapped in a hiplength fur coat.

"Fancy that," Nigel said, staring at Natasha. Lee had not greeted them or even betrayed any recognition.

She pretended not to hear him. She was staring at the crowded road that was full of taxis and cars edging away from the theater. Her ears were singing with the beat of her blood. She felt lost and alone.

Nigel moved closer, lowering his voice. "Are you okay?" he whispered.

She nodded.

"He might have said hello or something," Nigel said.

"Why should he?" Natasha said, walking on. She would have liked to duck out on the idea of supper but Nigel insisted, and rather than have a prolonged argument, she went, in the end. She pretended to enjoy herself. It saved another argument with Nigel.

"Enjoyed yourself?" he asked her as he took her home.

"Very much," she said with pretended enthusiasm, and he looked delighted.

"There, I told you it would make you feel better. It always gives you a lift to have a night out."

"So it does," she said, smiling at him.

He came around and opened her passenger door and helped her out with a solicitous hand under her elbow. She almost had the feeling he was going to offer to carry her, and in a flash she realized that Nigel's whole attitude had changed toward her since he found out about the baby.

Nigel might consider himself sexually liberated but in some ways he was more conservative and old-fashioned than he wanted anyone to know. He thought in simple terms. Once he had seen Natasha as a potential bedmate and pursued her relentlessly. Now he saw her as a potential mother and treated her as if she was made of china.

It was all very simple, really. It was probably what made Nigel a wizard with advertising slogans. He thought in easy, digestible terms. He thought in slogans.

He didn't really think at all. Nigel came up to a situation like a blank computer. His mind did a lightning search of its computer banks and came up with the correct answer to the situation and Nigel reacted with hardly a split second pause, with all apparent spontaneity.

All the same, she looked at him with amused affection suddenly and reached up lightly to kiss his cheek in a sisterly way. "Thank you, Nigel."

He went pink. "Think nothing of it."

"You're a dear," Natasha said, smiling. She said good-night and walked toward the house. Nigel got back into his car and drove away, leaving with her a picture of his embarrassed, rather pleased face. That was another aspect of him she was beginning to suspect— Nigel *liked* to behave correctly in a given situation. Faced with a ravishing girl he gave a wolf whistle and tried to date her. Faced with Natasha's situation he was doing the right thing in another way, and pleased because he thought he was succeeding in this new role. What role, exactly, she wondered. Nanny? "Nigel knows best," he had said smugly, and no doubt he thought he did. She would hate to disillusion him.

She slept very deeply that night. When she got up she felt heavy and dull. She felt terrible all day. She couldn't put her finger on what was wrong. She just knew she felt strange.

The feeling persisted for several days. Nigel noticed and told her scoldingly to see a doctor. She would have to, sooner or later, but she wanted to put off the embarrassment for as long as possible.

On the Friday evening she was watching a film on television when someone knocked on the door.

The last person she expected to see was Lee Farrell. She looked at him nervously.

"How are you?" he asked, his face cool.

"Fine, thank you." She didn't want to see him again and her tone made that obvious.

He glanced past her blocking figure. "Aren't you going to invite me in?"

She hesitated and his quick look made her flush. Nodding, she stepped back.

He was wearing a pale gray suit, the material fine and smooth, the cut flattering to his loose-limbed body. She closed the door and watched him as he surveyed the television, one brow curving upward.

"Might we have this off?" he asked, and she hurried over to switch off the set.

"Did you enjoy the play the other night?" he asked as she straightened and turned.

"Yes, did you?" She was pleased with herself for answering so calmly. For some odd reason she did not feel calm. She knew her heightened color must be betraying her and she wished she could make her face as cool as her voice.

"Not much," he said, the dart of those hard gray eyes disturbing.

"Oh?" she faltered, frowning.

"It bored me stiff," he said. "I wasn't in the mood for brittle comedy."

Neither had she been, Natasha thought, remembering her own mood that night. Had he felt like that? In a funny way, they were both accident victims. She hadn't seen it from his point of view before. No doubt he felt rather uneasy about the whole thing, too, although she had made no financial demands on him.

"You were with that fool Herries," he said, almost in accusation.

"We were with a party of friends," she said in tacit defense.

"God knows how you put up with the idiot."

"I work for him," she said. "I'm his secretary."

His mouth twisted and a disgusted expression came into the gray eyes. "I see," was all he said however. It was the way he said it that made her color burn.

"Nigel's a friend, nothing more." Until very recently he hadn't even been that, she thought. Now, he was, in a weird sort of way.

He looked around the room, his broad shoulders stiff with tension. "Eaten yet?"

She hesitated a shade too long. She should have answered at once and claimed to have done so. He caught her eye and she found herself reluctantly shaking her head.

"Have dinner with me," he said offhandedly, and she was abruptly irritated.

"No, thank you, I don't think so." If he had phrased it less curtly she might have agreed, but she reacted without thinking to the tone of his voice.

"Why not?" he demanded, his eyes darkening. "You spent an evening with that fool—you can spend one with me."

"I'm not hungry," she said, adding quickly, "But it's very kind of you. I'm sorry."

"Do you have to talk to me like that?" he asked in a rough voice, staring at her.

"Like what?"

"You talk to me as though I was dangerous. Do you

think I can't feel it—a damned great wall of ice between us everytime I look at you?"

"I'm sorry, I didn't mean—"

"You don't know what you mean," he said violently. "You blame me, don't you?"

"No," she protested, her color deepening gain.

"Oh, yes, I can sense it. It takes two, you know."

"I'm aware of that!"

"But you still can't bear to talk to me, can you?" he challenged, those darkened gray eyes probing into her. "You still blame me, whatever you say."

"I don't blame you," Natasha denied. "I just feel it would be best if we didn't see each other."

"Why?"

"Where's the point?" she asked him, and he moved restlessly, his face angry and flushed.

"I'm involved in this, whether you like it or not. You want to shut me out, pretend it has nothing to do with me. I've never been against the women's liberation movement, but you're taking it to ridiculous extremes. I'm prepared to accept that as you're the one actually having the baby you have to make most of the decisions about it, but I have some stake in it, too, you know. Like it or not, I am involved. You can't just ignore me."

Natasha sat down. It was that or fall down, and she felt the former alternative was more dignified. Her body was trembling violently. She said faintly, "Sit down, Mr. Farrell."

"Lee!" he exploded, his voice shooting up to the ceiling. "For God's sake—my name is Lee. You can't go on calling me Mr. Farrell like the young bride in a Victorian novel."

"Sorry," she said, then gave a faintly hysterical giggle as what he said sank home. It was rather absurd.

He sat down, his hands on his knees, staring at her across the space between them.

"Can't we just talk?" he asked, and Natasha sighed.

"What do you imagine we have to talk about?"

"We're two adult human beings. Are you telling me you can't imagine a subject we could discuss politely for a few hours?"

She looked up, a smile trembling around the corners of her mouth. "I still don't see the point, Mr.—Lee. Wouldn't it be best if we didn't see each other?"

"Why?" he attacked directly, his stare determined.

"Because we have nothing in common," Natasha said.

"How do you know until we've talked? The only time we've ever spent together we didn't do much talking."

She looked down, blushing angrily. "There you go again. I don't want to remember that night."

"I can see that all too plainly. How the hell do you think you're going to forget it? How the hell do you think I am?"

Natasha frowned, staring at her own hands as though she had never seen them before, tracing the fine blue network of veins buried deep under her pale skin.

"We're in the most intimate situation possible between a man and woman, yet you want to go on treating me as though I was a perfect stranger," he said curtly.

She bit her lip, not looking up.

"Can't you let that wall crash, Natasha?" Lee asked with faint humor in his deep voice.

"I don't want you to think—" She stopped dead, her face hot and confused, unable to go on.

"Think what?" he encouraged.

"That I'm—" She still couldn't say it, her voice faltering away with the sentence unfinished.

His eyes narrowed on her. She felt the pierce of their stare, and shrank. "An easy lay?" he demanded tersely, and she drew a shaky breath.

"Yes," she whispered.

"I don't think anything of the kind," he told her in a low, harsh voice. "You can get that out of your head. I'm not here in the hope of talking you into bed again, if that's what you think."

"Why are you here?" She looked at him through her lashes, her face worried. "If we're being frank—you can't blame me for being dubious about you. Apart from what happened between us, there's a lot of gossip about you, isn't there? Women like Lara Brennan—"

His brows met. "Lara? If you're asking if it is true that I've had an affair with her, yes. I have. I'm thirty-seven years old. I'm not a schoolboy. There have been women in my life from time to time. I'm not apologizing for having the normal sexual instincts."

"I didn't ask you to," she said, looking at him crossly.

"I'm glad about that," he said with sarcasm. "I came tonight because you're on my mind, I suppose. What do you expect? This situation is new to me. It was new from the start. The night we met I felt instinctively that this time was different, you were different. It all seemed dreamlike and inevitable."

"Yes," she said, struck by her own memories of that night and the fact that that was how she had felt.

"When you told me the next day about Porter and why you had gone off with me like that I was bitterly

angry. I felt—'' He broke off, his mouth tightening.
"Never mind, that's irrelevant. Nobody likes being used
for someone else's purposes, particularly when their
own emotions are involved." He smiled coldly at her.
"And no man likes to be told a woman went to bed with
him just to punish some other man."

"I wasn't punishing Mike—it wasn't like that."

"I had the feeling you didn't know why you had done
it," he said shrewdly. "You behaved like a typical
woman. You rushed off and threw your bonnet over the
windmill and then began to wish you hadn't."

She laughed angrily.

"Am I close?" he asked mockingly.

"Something like that," she agreed.

"As the windmill concerned, I feel I have some right
to a grievance," he said, and she was forced into a smile
again.

"That's better," he said. "That was the first thing I
noticed about you—the way you smile. You were laughing the first time I looked at you. You haven't laughed
much since, though."

"I haven't had much to laugh about," Natasha said
dryly.

He nodded, watching her with an unreadable expression. "Is it definitely all over with Porter?"

She sobered, nodding.

"No way back at all?" he asked, and she quietly told
him about Mike's mother. He listened intently, his face
betraying none of his thoughts.

"Tough luck," he said when she fell into silence.
"But if you'll excuse my saying so, he wasn't much of a
man if he let his mother run his life for him like that."
He glanced at his watch. "You still care for him?" he

asked casually, and Natasha didn't answer. She felt
him looking at her but didn't meet his eyes. "It's
rather late," he said. "But we could have a light supper somewhere, couldn't we? Now that we've broken
the ice?"

On impulse she stood up. "Thank you. I'll get a
jacket." She didn't know what she had been making
all that fuss about. He was right. Why shouldn't they
see each other politely now and then?

They had supper at an Italian restaurant. Although
it was late the place was crowded, as it was Friday
night. There was a small group playing there on a tiny
area of the floor, the lively crash of their music making
it only possible to hear if they half shouted at each
other.

They ate melon and ham, followed by a spaghetti
with an onion, tomato and bacon sauce. They talked
and smiled at each other and slowly Natasha found
herself totally relaxed, enjoying herself. Their conversation wandered from books to music to the theater, and
if their opinions clashed it was without heat, a lively
understanding growing between them as they explored
each other's tastes. Natasha had liked him the night she
first met him purely on sight. Most women would, she
thought, glancing at him secretively through her lashes.
He was a man with a strong sexual magnetism, less
because of the undoubted good looks and physical
power one saw at a glance than because of the assertive
masculinity in those gray eyes, the force of his per-
sonality.

"Enjoyed it?" he asked as he dropped her at her flat
much later that night.

"Yes," she said, her eyes smiling.

He brushed her cheek with one long lazy finger. "I won't say I told you so."

"No, don't do that," she said, amused.

"That revival of *She Stoops to Conquer* we were talking about," he said. "Like to see it? I'll get tickets. Next weekend?"

Natasha hesitated for a beat of time and his gray eyes skewered her with pointed humor.

"Don't say no," he ordered, smiling.

"I'm not allowed to?" Natasha asked.

He shook his head firmly. "No way. I'll get them."

She did not know if it was madness or pure reason but she did know she wanted to go, so she gave in with a smile. "Thank you."

"Good girl," he said complacently as she got out of the car. She was still smiling as she climbed into bed half an hour later. She felt happier than she had for weeks. It was a good feeling. She switched out the light, knowing she was going to sleep soundly, and fell into a deep sleep at once.

She enjoyed the evening at the theater, a week later, too. And the trip to the ballet he fixed the following week. Now and then over the ensuing weeks she made token protests about the regular dates they were having. She was uneasy about it. She did not want to come to rely on him. It was all too easy when someone was always around to find yourself growing attached to them. Although they had never discussed his private life, she imagined that Lee was still seeing Lara Brennan and, for all she knew, had other women in his life, too. He never laid a finger on Natasha. There was nothing remotely personal of that nature between them. He treated her more as if she were a sister or a friend. That was very reassuring in some ways, especially at the start, but at times she felt a bristling impatience when he treated her soothingly or humored her in case she burst into childish tears.

Lee felt guilty about her, she imagined. He hadn't said so, but she guessed that was behind his insistence on keeping tabs on her like this. He felt responsible for her, which was very kind of him, but Natasha wished sometimes she had never seen him again after that night they had spent together. For some reason, his presence in her life complicated it. She couldn't say why.

CHAPTER SEVEN

ONE MORNING WHEN SHE GOT UP she had that weird floating feeling again. She had had it once or twice early in her pregnancy and it had gone away. Now it was back. It stayed this time. She had lost her appetite. She was losing weight rather than gaining it, and her face was pale all the time. She wasn't sure if she was imagining it, but she knew she was not imagining the dizziness that came over her sometimes. She would bend over the filing cabinet at work and feel the room swim around her. Her vision would cloud. She would straighten, her ears singing with the beat of her own blood, and hang on to the edge of the metal drawer she was searching through, fighting off a sick faintness that only ebbed after a few minutes.

Natasha had fainted quite often in her teens. Some people never faint at all. Others do it at the drop of a hat. Natasha hated the feeling. She recognized it now, the threat of a loss of consciousness, the clouding of her sight and mind. There was something terrifying about feeling you were going to faint. Whenever she went to a dentist she always preferred to have a local anesthetic rather than gas—the idea of losing awareness was horrifying to her.

When it happened in Nigel's office he was very concerned. "Sit down. What's wrong? You're deathly white. What is it?'' he asked, pushing her into a chair.

She put her head down between her knees, shaking, and it was a minute or two before she was able to sit up again.

"You're ill," Nigel said nervously. "You must see a doctor."

"I will," Natasha agreed, but with reservation. She would only do that if she had to, and she hoped this strange sensation was going to pass as quickly as it had come.

Nigel have her a funny look. "Shouldn't you be... getting a bit fatter?" he asked with an embarrassed expression.

"Not yet," Natasha told him, mentally crossing her fingers. She had no idea whether she should or not, but she knew she was losing weight although she hadn't weighed herself. Her clothes were looser on her than they had been. She told herself that that was because she wasn't eating. She was skipping meals, not because she was dieting but because she often couldn't face the thought of food. The very idea of it made her want to throw up.

"Look, I'll ring a doctor," Nigel said anxiously.

"No, don't bother. I'll see mine tonight."

"You will?" he stressed, staring at her.

"You're fussing, Nigel," Natasha said, forcing a smile.

"I'm worried about you," he said. "You just don't look well."

"I'm fine," she said, but as she went home on the bus that evening she felt so terrible she thought she would pass out there and then. Luckily it was Saturday next day. She wouldn't have to force herself to get up at seven in order to rush to work. She could take it easy all day. She had never realized what a hectic pace she had to keep up all day until now. She had to leave for the office at just after eighty-thirty and she didn't get home again until getting on for seven, by which time she was often so tired and sick she couldn't eat even if she felt hungry. The weekends were much easier. She stayed in bed until ten or even eleven if she felt like it and she rested if she felt dizzy.

That Saturday she did her shopping in the morning and forced down a light meal of scrambled egg before she went out again for a slow walk along the river. Summer was over. The trees were stripping for winter, their gaudy leaves tossed on the fast-running river and borne away down to the sea. Gulls perched on the masts of ships and gave harsh quarreling cries to each other. The white concrete blocks of offices had the glitter of icebergs in the autumn sunshine. Natasha wandered without hurry, her eyes on the sky and water, her mind beset with anxiety. She hadn't yet breathed a hint to her family. So far there was no outward sign, but she knew it wouldn't be long before people began to notice, to whisper, to suspect. How was she going to stand it? The idea of being the center of a scandal made her ill.

There was a line of traffic jamming the road beside her. She glanced idly at it and her nerves flickered with fire as she saw Lee in a taxi. He wasn't looking her way. He was leaning sideways, his black hair gleaming with sunlight on it, and beside him sat Lara Brennan in a smart black jersey dress with a matching jacket. She was talking excitedly, her face alight, and as Natasha watched dully Lara flung her arms around Lee and kissed him. She turned away, shaking, her eyes blurred by a strange inky darkness that made her blind to where she was going. She walked straight into a lamp post, staggered on around it, the thundering in her head growing louder until it vanished.

The next she knew she was moaning with closed eyes. She couldn't remember what had happened. Her eyes lifted, dazed by the autumn sunlight. There were people standing all around her. She didn't look at their faces but she saw the shapes of them dimly. Her eyes moved around, alarm and embarrassment in them, and focused on Lee's frowning face.

"What happened?" he asked, and Natasha was so appalled by seeing him that she hurriedly shut her eyes again and pretended she hadn't heard.

"She passed out," someone said.

"Fainted dead away," agreed someone else.

"Someone ought to ring for an ambulance," another voice said.

"I'll take her to a doctor." That was Lee, his tone hard and firm, pushing aside the little argument that broke out between the members of the crowd who couldn't decide whether she ought to be moved or not.

Lee ended it by picking her up firmly, a hand under her back, another under her knees, and carrying her to his taxi. She would have protested and told him to put her down if she had had the strength, but those dizzying swooping sensations had hold of her again. She couldn't do anything but hold on. She felt like someone on a dipper at a fairground.

Lee put her down in a corner of the back of the taxi. She heard the engine chugging, the vehicle shuddering. The door slammed. A husky, smoky voice asked, "What happened?"

"She fainted," Lee said, very close to Natasha.

"Where to, guv?" a hoarse male voice asked. "The hospital?"

"No," Lee said. "I'll get a doctor for her later. The same address as before." The taxi moved off and Lee added, "I'll drop you on the way to my house." Natasha wasn't sure if he was speaking to her or to the other girl, but she couldn't open her eyes yet. She felt cold, icily cold. Her hands and feet seemed to have no blood in them at all. Her face had the pinched chill of starvation.

"Looks terrible, doesn't she?" The other girl moved, her body rustling, an expensive perfume wafting toward Natasha's nostrils. "White as a sheet. Did you say you knew her?"

"Yes, she's a friend," Lee said, and there was a gurgle of laughter.

"Oh, yes?" Natasha hated the soft tease in that voice, the mocking insinuation.

"Yes," Lee said with faint grimness.

"I'd better come along in case you need help with her," Lara Brennan said. The taxi had slowed and was stopping.

"No, I'll cope," Lee said.

"Sure?"

"Quite sure, thanks."

"Oh, well, you know best." Lara sounded faintly resentful though. She got up. The seat gave, the springs creaking. There was the soft, unmistakable sound of a kiss. "Be good," Lara said in her husky, mocking voice. "I hope your—" she paused, her voice even more mocking "—your friend. . .is okay. I'd get her to a doctor fast if I were you. She looks as if she could do with a blood transfusion. You haven't turned vampire, have you, Lee?''

The door slammed before Lee could answer that. The taxi started off again and Natasha felt Lee shift beside her. As they took a corner her body swayed and he put an arm around her. Natasha pulled away, stiffening.

She forced up her lips. Lee was staring at her, his black brows a heavy line across the gray eyes.

"How do you feel now?" he asked huskily, and she somehow managed to force a smile.

"Better."

"You don't look better," he said with explosive impatience. "You look terrible. What the hell have you been doing to get yourself into that state?"

"I fainted, that's all." She was slightly resentful. She didn't want him shouting at her. She felt too weak for that vibrant male aggression of his at the moment.

"How long have you been like this?" She hadn't seen him for ten days but he sounded as though it was ten months, his voice bristling.

"Only today," she lied, because she was frightened to admit the feeling had been growing on her for about a week. Sometimes you reach a point where you have faced all you can face. Natasha had done that when she first realized she was pregnant. She had been marking time since then, gathering strength with which to face a lot of other things, like telling her family and making arrangements about having the baby. She couldn't quite face the physical sickness she had been having this week. She was blindly afraid of what it might be. She lay awake worrying about it, but she couldn't bring herself to go to a doctor. She was too scared of what she might hear.

"Only today?" Lee probed, and his voice said he didn't believe her. Her eyes slid nervously away from those sharp gray eyes.

Her silence made Lee lean closer, his voice hard and tense. "I could slap you. You're the most obstinate—" His voice broke off as she trembled. "Oh, hell," he said under his breath.

The taxi stopped. Lee paid the driver and turned to get Natasha out of the seat. She had already slid across and was stumbling out on her own two feet. Lee put an arm around her waist. She half protested, then gave in, her legs still weak under her.

It wasn't until Lee had guided her into the house that she noticed her surroundings. While he was steering her across a wide, white-ceilinged hall that gave an impression of space and light and luxury, she was concentrating on staying upright but she was taking in the impression the hall made at first glance.

Lee pushed her down on to a long couch. He looked at her, his body tense with suppressed irritation. "I won't be a minute. Stay put!"

She didn't answer. He walked out of the room. She heard him dialing, then his voice talking. Natasha did not listen. She was staring around the room guardedly, curiously.

It was furnished in a comfortable fashion between the ultramodern and the timeless classical furniture that does not date. The carpet was deep-piled, oaten in color. The curtains were a heavy golden velvet. A bowl of russet chrysanthemums stood on a smoked glass table near the window. The couch on which Natasha was sitting was a cream linen-covered rectangle piled high with buttoned cushions. An elaborate stereo bank stood along one wall, the chromium buttons on the panel glittering in the sunlight.

Lee came back with a glass of water and made her drink some. "I've called the doctor," he told her. "I rang mine. He's a friend. He'll be here in two minutes."

He hadn't exaggerated. Natasha had hardly finished her water when the doctor came into the room. He was a young man with flat blond hair and a face like a rabbit, but he was very pleasant and she didn't feel threatened. He made no comment until he had finished examining her. As he folded his stethoscope back into his bag he called, "Lee, you can come back now."

Lee walked slowly into the room, looking sharply at Natasha, then glanced at the doctor, raising one brow. "Well?"

"I can't be certain until we've done some tests, but I think we're going to run into some trouble," the doctor said, snapping his case shut.

"What sort of trouble?"

"Hard to say for sure until—" the doctor began, and Lee broke in tersely.

"Force yourself, James. You've got some ideas. What's wrong with her?"

He got a wry look. "You want me to stick my neck out on pure guesswork? I could be way out."

"We'll take that risk. Give us your own off-the-cuff opinion. We won't ask for our money back if you're wrong."

The young man laughed. "From what she has told me, then, I think she may lose the baby."

"Oh!" Natasha cried involuntarily. She hadn't let herself form the suspicion. It had been there at the back of her mind, and now that it had been put into words she knew how much she did not want to lose the baby, how badly she would feel if she did.

The doctor looked at her quickly. "Don't get worried. I said you may lose it—I didn't say you were going to. If you do as you're told there's no reason why you should." He looked at Lee again. "Rest," he said. "She has got to rest. There's an instability there that worries me. She's very thin and from the look of her I'd say the baby isn't growing as it should. She must go to bed and stay there until she's told she can get up. No work. No worries. Rest and peace of mind is what she needs for the next few months if she isn't to lose the baby."

Natasha lay back, trembling. Lee asked brusquely, "What do you mean, instability?"

"With the pregnancy," the doctor said. "She isn't very strong. It won't be easy. I'll set up the tests right away. She ought to come into the hospital to have them. I'll be in touch when I've made all the arrangements."

He hurriedly scribbled on a pad and tore off the sheet, handing it to Lee. "Iron and vitamins. She's anemic. Make sure she takes them." He walked to the door and Lee followed him, giving Natasha a brief look as he went.

She stared at nothing, her eyes fixed in blank introspection. She felt guilty. She should have gone to a doctor sooner. She had known something was wrong right from the start. She hadn't been certain but she had guessed, anyway.

Lee came back and looked at her from across the room. "You'll stay here tonight," he said in a tone that refused to admit of any discussion.

Natasha said weakly, "I can't."

"You can go to bed now," Lee said, ignoring her. He came over and picked her up like a child.

"I can't," Natasha said, her lip trembling.

He carried her up the stairs and she talked at the hard line of his jaw, which was all she could see with her head against his shoulder. "I can rest in bed in my flat. I can't stay here. I can't stay in bed every day, anyway, not every day. I've got to work. Put me down, Lee."

"Give me the key of your flat and I'll fetch your things," he said as though she hadn't spoken at all.

"Did you hear what I said?" she demanded, stirring as she was laid down on a bed.

Lee sat on the edge of the bed, the springs giving, and before she realized what he intended had begun to undo the green shirt she wore. Natasha pushed his hands away, gasping. "What do you think you're doing?" Hot color had rushed into her face.

"I'm taking off your clothes," he said with a dry smile. "And don't get carried away with excitement because I've no designs on you, and I won't be filled with lust at the sight of you without them."

"I can take them off myself," she said crossly.

He got up and strolled to the door. "I'll give you two minutes, then I'll be back to make sure you're doing what you're told."

She hesitated only for a second then she hurriedly began pulling off her clothes. When he opened the door again she was in the bed with the covers pulled up to her neck.

He surveyed her with a mocking smile. "Very modest," he taunted. Holding out a hand he said, "Key, please."

"In my jacket pocket," she muttered.

"Graciously said," Lee said, finding it. "Now, you will stay just where you are. You will not get dressed again. You will not get out of that bed."

"This is ridiculous," Natasha said, glaring at him. "I'm not a child."

"I wouldn't place any bets on it," he said, walking to the door.

When he had gone she lay looking around the room. It was pink and white, an apple blossom room, very feminine and pretty. She couldn't stay, she thought. Lee didn't really want her here. Why should he? She had seen the way he reached for Lara when the other woman put her arms around his neck and kissed him. They knew each other very well. Natasha had heard the intimacy in their voices, seen it in their faces. Lee was being kind because he felt responsible for her, just as he might have done if he really had run her down with his car, except that what had happened had been more her fault than his—she had jaywalked in front of him and he couldn't be blamed if it had been a disaster for her.

It was her own fault. If she didn't feel so ill she would get up and dress and go, but she closed her eyes on a wave of dim weakness, admitting to herself that she was ill. She could not bring herself to get out of that bed and go home.

She heard Lee's quick, confident footsteps on the stairs and her heart leaped inside her like a stranded fish, leaving her breathless and shaken.

He came into the room and his gray eyes flashed to her face. "You're looking better already," he said in surprise. "Far more color."

The color had crawled into her face when she heard

him coming but she pushed the admission out of her mind.

"I could go home now," she said, her hands clasping the sheet to hold it up to her chin.

"You could not," Lee told her. He put a suitcase down on the floor. "I got your things."

"Oh," she said, lips parted in astonishment. "You were quick."

He opened the case and hunted through the neatly folded piles of clothes. "Here," he said, tossing a short cotton nightie onto the bed. "Get into this."

She lay stiffly in mute apprehension, watching him, her fingers tightening on the sheet. He stood there, staring at her with suddenly grim eyes. When he moved she flinched.

"Stop it!" he said tightly, bending over her and deepening her odd anxiety.

"Stop what?"

"Stop working yourself up into hysteria because I'm in a bedroom with you and you're naked under that sheet," he said contemptuously.

She looked up at him, confused and huge-eyed. "I'm not."

"Oh, yes, you are. You always are when I'm around. You jump if I so much as put a finger on you. Do you think I haven't noticed? You get a look of panic whenever I'm within ten feet of you."

"You aren't making me feel any better by shouting at me," Natasha whispered, clutching the sheet tighter.

"I'm not shouting," he roared.

She cringed against the pillows and he sat down on the edge of the bed, his eyes flashing with fury. As he reached toward her she gave a smothered cry of panic.

His hand wrenched the sheet away, pulling it violently from her tethering fingers. She grabbed for it again and it was whisked down out of her reach while Lee's brilliant, dark-pupiled stare roamed down over her pale body in unhidden exploration.

She froze into a statue under that look, her lips parted in a hastily drawn breath. "Stop it," she whispered, trembling.

"Why the hell should I?" he muttered without looking up at her face. As he put out a hand to touch her she tried to push him away, a frantic fear filling her. She had not felt like this the night they first met. Now she felt nervous, afraid, shaken, because the roving sexual appraisal she was getting aroused a terrified response inside her and she was scared of letting Lee touch her again. She couldn't bear the thought of having him make love to her. A great black wall came down inside her mind at the very idea.

Lee caught her wrist and pushed her arm back firmly yet with insistence. He leaned over her, pinioning her to the bed with the weight of his body. "What are you so scared of?" he muttered thickly. "You weren't scared that night. Stop looking at me as if I'm some sort of monster."

"Let me go," she said weakly, staring up into his darkened eyes, then her whole body stiffened as she felt his warm hand touch her naked breast, his palm cupping it, his long fingers smoothly stroking upward. Her nipple hardened under his fingertips and Natasha's eyes closed helplessly. A second later Lee's mouth was touching hers and a sigh wrenched her as her senses vibrated in wild response. Her free hand crept up his arm, touched his throat, his hair. The demanding bruising of his kiss became warm, gentle, coaxing, and his hand slid from her breast to follow the silken curve of her hip.

Lee pulled himself away, drawing a long shuddering breath, and looked down at her flushed face, his lids half cloaking the darkened eyes.

"You see?" he asked in a low, husky voice, giving her a crooked little smile. "Not so terrifying after all, was it? You're quite safe under my roof, Natasha. I want you. I won't pretend I don't. But I'm not inclined to fantasies of rape, and you can sleep in this bed alone without being afraid I'll come bursting in through the door and leap on you before you can scream the place down." He stood up and handed her the nightie while she lay there, unable to meet his eyes. "Just stop bolting for cover every time I come near you," he said as he walked away to the door.

He halted, his back to her. "Could you eat something?"

"No, thank you," she whispered like a polite child, shaking from head to foot.

"Some tea or coffee?"

"No, thank you. I'll just get some sleep," she said, swallowing.

He went out and closed the door and she fumbled herself into the nightie and lay down, pulling the covers over her again. She was sick with self-hatred. She knew that while Lee was holding her, kissing, caressing her, she had been craving far more than what he was actually doing, and she despised herself. Lee had been showing her that he could kiss her without going any further, that she was absolutely safe in his house. She had been past caring. If she had invited him to go on, no doubt he would have done so. She wasn't so inexperienced that she had been unaware of his sexual desire for her. Nor was she deceived into imagining it meant anything more than a normal male's response to having an attractive girl naked in his arms. If she had let Lee take her again she would have been drowning in self-contempt afterward. At least last time she could tell herself she was unhappy and desperate and very much influenced by champagne. This time she had no such excuses. This time she had been weak at the thought of Lee's lovemaking. She had longed to have him go on. She had wanted him with an aching desire she still felt deep inside her body.

CHAPTER EIGHT

SHE HAD THE TESTS three days later. She only spent a day
in the hospital and then Lee took her back to his house,
despite her protests. The results of the tests came
through next day. Lee's friend, James, came and sat in
the comfortable bedroom and took her hand, smiling at
her.

"We think you'll do," he said teasingly.

Natasha looked hopefully at him. "I'm not going to
lose the baby?"

"If you're very good and do what you're told, no,"
he said. "We want you to stop work at once and stay in
bed most of the time until about the sixth month. By
then the danger period should be well past."

She stared at him, paling. "But, I can't—"

His forehead creased. "I'm afraid you're going to
have to, Natasha. It is very important you follow our
orders exactly."

"She will," Lee said curtly. He had been sitting there,
listening, his face hard.

Natasha glanced nervously at him. James stood up,
smiling. "Be a sensible girl," he advised, "and everything will be fine. You want the baby, don't you?"

She nodded. Oh, yes, she wanted it. She had lived
with it as a fact for months. She had resisted the idea of
it at first, but it had crept up on her in oblique, crablike

ways over the past weeks. Questions dropped into her mind when she was sitting alone. What would it look like? Would it be a boy or a girl? How could you help wondering, half imagining the reality that was yet unglimpsed? The ripening seed inside her would one day be a human being, a child, her child, and she already knew a wondering interest in it. The idea of losing it now made her suffer.

Lee walked out with James and came back alone. He stood staring at her as she fixed her disturbed eyes on the wall.

Slowly she said, "I suppose I'll have to go to my parents' home." What choice did she have? She could not keep her flat and herself when she was no longer working.

"No," Lee said, and she looked at him in bewildered surprise.

"I've have to. I can't see any other way."

"This clinches it," Lee said brusquely. "You're marrying me."

She looked at him in shock. "No," she said at once, without even thinking, her voice raw with pain. She could not bear it.

Lee looked at her with a bitter anger. "Don't argue. My mind's made up."

"*Your* mind—don't try to give me orders, push me around," she burst out, trembling with anger and hurt.

"We both know that's the way it is going to be," he said through tight lips. "Look in a mirror. You've gone white. You know you can't face your parents. Some girls could walk in cool as a cucumber and say, 'Guess what, mum and dad, I'm expecting.' But not you, Natasha. You're sitting there screwing yourself up into agony at the very idea of it. You have the look of someone getting ready to jump off a cliff. I'm not standing by and seeing you put yourself through mental torture when I can so easily stop it.''

"We've been through all this before," she said miserably. "You don't want to marry me.''

"What either of us wants is beside the point," he said harshly, then he looked at her fixedly, his face hard and unreadable, the lines of it get in grim thought. "I'll make a bargain with you," he said slowly. "We get married. You have the baby. Then if you want to—we get a divorce. That solves both the problem of the immediate future and the doubts you have about getting married at all. We'll make it a matter of pure convenience. The minute either of us wants out . . . we say so.''

Natasha looked away, frowning. Her mind struggled to come to a decision. It was tempting. How could she deny that? Lee was right, of course. It solved her immediate problems. It raised many others, of course, but they were not so immediate, and she was reluctant to face them anyway at this moment.

"Is it a bargain?" Lee asked brusquely.

She looked at him, biting her lip. After a moment she nodded. "If you're sure you aren't going to resent offering," she added with a wry little smile.

"I'm sure," he said, his mouth crooked, glancing away. "Do you want to invite your family to the wedding?"

She hurriedly shook her head. A short time ago the very idea of getting married without even telling her parents would have shaken her to the roots. She knew they were bound to be bitterly hurt and worried and puzzled, but this marriage was not a real marriage. It was a sham, a pretense, a phony, and Natasha did not want her family to be present. She could not bear the idea of seeing their faces, pretending in front of them, putting on the bright smiles of a happy bride.

She met Lee's cool gray eyes and saw in them his comprehension of her reason for refusing. He had read her mind accurately, his face grim.

"Right," he said, without comment, though. "Now, you can't be left alone in the house all day and I will have to get back to work soon. I'm going to have someone living in—an old friend of mine. Lucy Truscot—she was at school with my mother. She's widowed and sometimes works part-time for me, more to keep herself occupied than to earn money. She'll keep an eye on you and run the house."

"I don't want you to make new arrangements just on my account," Natasha protested, her face distressed. "I don't want to upset your life. I feel guilty enough already."

"There's no occasion for you to feel guilty. Lucy will be happy to do it."

"But—" she began, and he cut in tersely.

"Don't argue. I've made up my mind."

She sat upright, her bare smooth shoulders very pale against the blue nightdress she was wearing. "Must you ride roughshod over me? What makes you think you can just make decisions for me, as though I was a child? You might at least make a pretense of discussing it."

"All right," he said, sitting down on the bed with an impatient sigh. "We'll discuss it. I want to have someone here because if I have to go out for hours, leaving you alone in the house, I will worry and be unable to concentrate on my work."

Natasha stared at him, lips parted.

He viewed her dryly, one brow lifted. "Your turn," he said with grim mockery. "What do you say to that?"

She shifted in the bed restlessly. "What *can* I say? I appreciate it."

"Gracious as ever," he murmured, his mouth twisting.

"I'm sorry," she said. "Thank you, I'm grateful and I'm sorry if I was *ungrateful*."

He smiled at her, amusement in his gray eyes. "So I should think. Can we make another bargain, do you think?"

Natasha looked warily at him. "What sort of bargain?"

"Will you stop questioning everything and just accept that for the moment we're involved together? I realize you're unwilling to accept anything from me, but circumstances are against you, Natasha. Like it or not, you're going to be my wife and you're going to have to stay in bed for several months, at least. Try to be patient, try to stop arguing."

He smiled at her again, his mouth wry. "Okay?"

"Okay," she said, giving a long sigh. What else could she say?

James visited her again on the following day to make sure she was following instructions, he said, grinning at her. He sat on the edge of the bed and listened to the baby's heartbeat for a moment, then sat up and said, "Sound as a drum. Don't worry. He's in there."

"Or she," Natasha reminded him.

"Is he being sexist?" Lee asked, coming into the room.

"I plead guilty," James told him with a wicked smile.

"But I got my wrists slapped. Don't worry, though. It is doing fine."

"We're getting married," Lee told him. "Is it okay for Natasha to get out of bed for an hour?"

"No longer," James insisted. "And keep her sitting down as much as you can. Am I invited, by the way?" He showed no flicker of surprise or curiosity and Natasha, aware that she was very flushed, liked him the more for that.

"Of course, but no plated toasters for a wedding present, if you don't mind," Lee said casually.

"I was thinking of a washing line," James said, snapping shut his case and standing up.

"A what?" Lee began to laugh.

"Useful present," James told him. "You can tie Natasha in the bed with it and then after the baby has arrived it will come in handy for hanging out the nappies."

" Nappies?" Lee repeated with a grimace.

"Babies will wear them," James said, grinning at Natasha. "Look out, he's wondering if he ought to change his mind. There's something about nappies that is very off-putting."

"No such thing," Lee denied, but with a smile.

"I don't see it," James said, considering him.

"What don't you see?" asked Lee, one dark brow curving upward in a sardonic line.

"You changing a baby's nappy."

"Neither," said Lee wryly, "do I!" He turned and looked at Natasha, his eyes smiling. "You won't demand that of me, will you? I'm a reasonable man, but I have to draw the line somewhere and I'm afraid nappies is it."

"I'll remember that," she promised, smiling back. "I gather James isn't the only one around here with sexist attitudes? If women had a union—"

Lee interrupted her, his face filled with amusement. "If men had a union, you mean—we would demand demarcation lines and you can be pretty certain that nappy changing would fall within your province."

James moved to the door, swinging his black case in one hand. "When is this wedding, anyway?"

Lee turned toward him. "I've just been making the arrangements. I've managed to fit in a quick civil ceremony for next Tuesday. At a quarter past eleven. Let me know if you can make it."

"I'll make it," James said as he walked out the door. "This I've got to see—you putting your head in a marital noose."

"Don't knock it—you haven't tried it yet," Lee told him, walking out of the room after him. Natasha heard their light, friendly voices as they went downstairs, and she listened without hearing what they said, her mind occupied in coming to terms with the casual way Lee had announced that he had actually fixed the time and date.

It was one thing to know that they had agreed to get married, but quite another to hear him say so calmly that it was all arranged. It brought the matter into new perspective. It made it real and settled and a mental fait accompli.

Natasha put her little finger to her lips and bit it anxiously, frowning.

She wasn't sure, either, that she liked the way Lee had phrased his announcement. He had managed to fit in a quick ceremony at a quarter past eleven, had he? Be-

tween his coffee break and his lunchtime, no doubt.
One of the little chores he had made a note of among all
the other daily routine. Get married, have lunch, board
meeting at three o'clock. She could just see it in his office diary.

She didn't expect any romantic phrases or baskets of
red roses, but there was something horribly humdrum
about the way he had tossed off the remark to James.
He hadn't even looked at her. He hadn't been telling her
at all. He had only mentioned the arrangement because
James asked. No doubt if James had not asked Lee
would have forgotten to mention it to her except
possibly on the actual morning over breakfast when he
might have said casually, "By the way, be at our wedding at a quarter past eleven, won't you?"

She heard him coming back and when he paused in
the doorway gave him an unrevealing smile. "Okay?"
Lee asked, and she said yes, she was fine, just fine. He
looked at her oddly, but said nothing. Perhaps he took
her at her word or perhaps, she thought gloomily, he
had only been polite when he asked and didn't really
care one way or the other.

She rang Nigel later that afternoon. Lee had already
been in touch with him to tell him Natasha was ill and
would not be coming to work for a while, but Natasha
felt she had to let Nigel know as soon as possible that
she would not be returning at all so that he could find a
replacement for her as soon as he could.

"How are you?" Nigel asked cheerfully.

"I feel much better," she said carefully, getting ready
to drop her bombshell, but Nigel went on without
waiting for her to add anything.

"That's fine. The place is a morgue without you. I've

even had to answer my phone myself. I'm fed up to the back teeth. When are you coming back?''

She launched into her apologetic explanation and he interrupted it in disbelief.

"You're what?''

"Getting married,'' she said huskily, glad he couldn't see her because she had gone bright pink.

"Who to?'' Nigel demanded, and she answered, her hesitant reply broken into by a shouted, "Lee Farrell? You're marrying Lee Farrell? You're kidding! I'd have sworn he wasn't the marrying kind. Wonders will never cease. It must be those big blue eyes of yours. Well, congratulations, darling.''

"Thank you,'' she said in a stiff voice.

Nigel was quiet for a second, then said gruffly, "Glad it worked out for you. It was tough. Some girls might weather it, but I wondered how you would.''

Natasha didn't say anything to that and after another pause Nigel said, "I went around to your flat with some grapes, actually. I did wonder where you were when I didn't get a reply.''

"I'm at Lee's house.''

"I see.'' Nigel sounded amused. "When's the wedding?''

"Next week.''

"Can I come?''

"Of course,'' Natasha said, wondering how Lee would react to the news that she had invited Nigel. But, after all, he had asked James, and even if it was a very quick civil wedding it would be nice to have someone she knew there.

When she told Lee he eyed her disgustedly. "That fool?''

"He can be very kind."

"He can be an idiot, too, and he usually is," Lee said with a dry note in his voice. "Anyone else you want to invite while we're at it?"

She shook her head. "There's no one."

Lee stared at her, his gray eyes enigmatic, but he made no comment. She wondered what he was thinking. That she had very few friends? Well, that was true enough. She had acquaintances, but she was not the outgoing type. She did not make friends easily and in London the people she did meet seemed on the move all the time. They came and they went, which was, no doubt, what was known as a floating population. London was a tidal city. People flooded in all the time and ebbed out again, leaving only the human driftwood of a few outsiders beached between tides.

"Sure you don't want to invite your family?" he asked. "They're bound to be hurt, you know."

"I know," she said, sighing. "But it would cause more trouble if I told them I was getting married in a hurry like this—I'd rather break it to them afterward and give them no chance to discuss it."

Lee studied her, his expression shrewd. "They might try to talk you out if it?"

She nodded. "I know what would happen. The minute I told them, my mother would start probing and asking questions. She would try to persuade me to have what she would call a proper wedding, a wedding with all the trimmings. And when I told her I couldn't wait for that she would know why."

Lee's mouth twisted grimly. "Natasha, she has to find out why sooner or later."

"I know," she said. "But this way will make it easier

for her, for them. They won't have to be there and pretend to be wildly happy while inside they are miserable."

He watched her. "I see. Maybe you're right."

The phone rang and he got up and went downstairs to answer it. "Lara!" she heard him say, his voice deep and warm and full of pleasure. Natasha felt a queer little twist of pain inside her. She hurriedly told herself it wasn't because she was jealous or hurt. It was because she realized she was ruining Lee's chances of happiness with Lara Brennan. Did he feel more for Lara than he admitted? His voice had sounded so pleased when he recognized her voice.

He had said coolly that he had had an affair with Lara. He had somehow left her with the feeling that the affair was over. His voice had made that impression. She had sensed he was using the past tense. But had she leaped to the wrong conclusion? They still saw a good deal of each other. She had seen Lara kiss him, heard her talking to him in a warm intimate voice, like the voice Lee was using at this moment downstairs.

"Lara, don't be absurd," he said, laughing, and Natasha bit her lower lip, struggling with burning tears. She heard the click of the receiver as he replaced it. She ran a trembling hand over her wet eyes, fighting down her tears as she heard him returning.

The bright smile she gave him didn't quite convince him. He stared at her sharply. "Something wrong?"

"No," she said in a light, artificial voice. "Who was that on the phone?"

"Why?" he asked even more sharply, his brows meeting.

She gave a pretense of a shrug. "I just wondered."

"It wasn't for you," he said in a terse voice, and Natasha looked at him directly then, surprise in her face.

"Wasn't that why you asked?" he demanded, his eyes darkening. "What are you hoping for? That Porter will realize he can't live without you and come to persuade you to go back to him?"

"No," she said, suddenly angry with him because he had mentioned Mike. She had shut off thoughts of Mike weeks ago. She did not want those painful memories resurrected. At first she had found the memory of Mike always returning whenever she relaxed her guard, but lately he had risen in her mind less and less. *It isn't always true,* she thought, *that absence makes the heart grow fonder. If you are fiercely determined you can root out love. It is a weed that can be burned out from the heart, but like most weeds, it has to be dealt with firmly.* Natasha might have forgotten those moral principles, which her parents had beaten into her head, for one night, but she had called on their strength to help her forget Mike. She had refused to let herself think about him, and gradually the strategy had begun to work.

"If Porter really loved you—" Lee began, and she cut him short, her face and voice angry.

"I don't want to discuss him."

"Do you think I don't know you still think about him?" Lee demanded, his powerful features tightly controlled but his voice vibrating with anger. "Every time you sit there with that blank expression on your face I know what's in your mind. Why don't you face it? He didn't love you enough to defy his mother, and you're wasting your time daydreaming about him."

"I'm not daydreaming about him!" There was a harshness in his voice that had hurt, and Natasha responded by snapping at him in her turn.

"Then what was wrong?" Lee asked in a curt voice, and she looked down, because she could not tell him the truth and she was afraid he might just pick up her true feelings from her expression. Natasha wasn't even certain what those feelings were. She had felt pain, but she did not quite know why. She was not emotionally involved with Lee Farrell, she pointed out to herself. She had no claims on him apart from having jaywalked into his life like some sleepwalker bent on self-destruction. Why should it matter to her if he talked to another woman with laughter and intimacy in his voice?

Lee strode over and sat down on the bed, one hand reaching out to take her throat, his fingers cool against her warm bare skin, turning her around to face him. It wasn't hurting. It was firm but gentle. Yet Natasha felt impelled to burst out, "Don't. Let me go."

His fingers tightened. She saw a flash of white-hot rage in his eyes. Then he pulled her head toward him and she began to breathe painfully as his mouth roughly found hers, the bruising pressure making her push at him resentfully. He was hurting her and she recognized that he was doing it deliberately. It was a punishment. Her attempt to get away made him even angrier. He framed her face between his hands and kissed her forcefully, not even trying to coax her. Natasha's hand curled in his shoulder, her fingers digging into him. She was so hurt, so angry, that she lost her temper and really began to fight, her arms thrusting him away, her head twisting and turning as she struggled in his grip.

She managed it at last. Lee's hands released her and

she fell back against her pillows, panting, a hand to her bruised, hot mouth. He sprang up and strode to the window, then stood there with his back to her, breathing audibly, his lean body taut, his hands gripping the windowsill in a violent grasp.

Natasha lay trembling in the bed, staring bitterly at the back of his head. "Don't ever...ever...touch me again," she said in a husky, low mutter. "I could not stand it."

Lee didn't answer or move for a minute or two. She heard his breathing slowing until at last, without looking at her, he turned and walked out of the room in silence.

CHAPTER NINE

LUCY TRUSCOT TOOK OVER THE HOUSE the following day. Natasha liked her on sight. It was easy to like Lucy. She had a face that smiled even when she was not smiling. Her eyes were full of warmth and she was interested in everyone and everything. Small and thin and quick, she went around the house like a sparrow hopping in the garden, chirping. She seemed to think that, being in bed all day, Natasha needed to have the news of what was going on outside in the world relayed to her at frequent intervals. Lucy's mission in life was to pass news on to anyone who would listen to her. Natasha was not going to get bored with Lucy around, that was obvious from the first morning.

"Cup of tea? They're doing up the road. Can you hear the drills? That's going to give us all a headache. I see they're painting the front of number thirty-four. Horrible color pink. What's that supposed to be, I asked the painter. Amethyst, he said. Amethyst! The things they think of. How about a nice piece of plaice for your lunch? I'll do it in a mushroom sauce. Good for the baby, milk and fish." While she talked she was darting around the bed tucking in the bedclothes, picking up a magazine that had fallen to the floor, adjusting the hang of the curtains. Lucy was never still and rarely silent.

"I like plaice," Natasha said shyly. "Thank you very much."

"There's the phone," Lucy said, flying to the door on her tiny, slippered feet. She had thin white hair that clustered in wisps on her forehead and her bright eyes were always alert. Natasha stared after her, wishing she could think of more to say in response to Lucy's stream of talk. It was always so hard to show you liked someone even though you hadn't much to say. You had to rely on smiles, and when you were as shy as Natasha it wasn't always easy to smile naturally.

Lucy came back. "It was Lee," she said, and Natasha looked at her nervously.

"Oh?" Why had he rung up?

"Just to make sure you were okay," Lucy said, removing her cup. "I told him you were fine. He worries too much. Always did as a boy. A perfectionist, always wanting things to be the way *he* wanted them. Well, I told him life's not like that. All very well being a dreamer, but sometimes you have to put your trust in other people."

Natasha frowned, confused. Lucy went out. What had all that meant, Natasha thought. Had Lucy meant that Lee should trust *her*? Lee—a dreamer? That didn't sound like him. He was far too sure of himself, far too sure he could make life do as he pleased, to give himself up to daydreams. Natasha was a daydreamer. Introverts often are. She spent a good deal of time lost in her own world and it was sometimes a shock to her to come out of it to find this parallel human world operating in a different way around her.

On the morning of her wedding she was getting dressed with Lucy's cheerful help when she heard someone knock at the door. It was not a polite rat-tat. It was more like someone battering the door with his fists, and Lucy looked up, her mouth open. "Whatever's that? What a racket. Sounds like trouble to me."

"I hope not," Natasha said, forcing a smile. She was feeling very sick and shaky. She had not been out of bed for days and her legs were not sure how to work anymore, she supposed. There had to be some reason why she was trembling as she tried to stand while Lucy zipped up her cream woolen dress.

It was a compromise dress. Lee had said offhandedly, "Wear white, for heaven's sake, why not?" Natasha couldn't have worn white. The very idea had made her wince. She had had this dress in the wardrobe. It was a slim-fitting, high-necked dress with short sleeves and a row of tiny buttons down the front.

Someone's voice was raised downstairs. Lucy put her head to one side, listening curiously. "Whoever is it? Someone's in a temper." She turned and Natasha was gripping the dressing table with both hands, her face dead white. "My dear girl, what's the matter? Quick, sit down. Are you going to faint? Merciful goodness, you're a color." Lucy guided her into the little bedroom chair and Natasha tried to pull herself together. *Mike's voice,* she thought. *What is he shouting at Lee? Why is he here? What is going on?*

Lucy was torn between a desire to know what was happening downstairs and a concern over Natasha's sudden whiteness. She crouched beside her, rubbing her ice-cold hands.

They both heard the crash of some heavy object hitting the floor. Then came scuffling sounds, thuds, followed by the banging of the front door.

"Gracious," Lucy said, half ready to fly out of the room. "Are you all right, dear? Do you want me to get the doctor?"

Natasha shook her head, wishing Lucy would be quiet so that she could concentrate on whatever was going on downstairs.

"Sure?" Lucy asked, ready to be convinced.

"I'm fine now," Natasha said. The noises downstairs had stopped. There was silence. What was happening now?

"I wonder what all that was about?" Lucy said, dying to go and see but feeling she should stay with Natasha, her small face full of conflicting ideas. She looked around. "Are you going to be fit enough to go through with everything? Would you rather put if off until you feel better?"

"No, I'm quite okay. I was a bit faint. Don't tell Lee—it would worry him." Natasha did not want to have to face this all over again. She was psychologically ready to go through with the wedding now. She knew that if she had another interval of waiting she would start getting cold feet and would want to get out of it altogether. Best to go on with it, get it over with.

Lee walked into the room. He was wearing an elegant dark suit with a crisp white shirt and a wine-colored tie. He might have been on his way to the office, Natasha thought, not on his way to get married. Neither of them looked as though they were going to do that. This was a farce, a black farce.

"Ready?" he asked coolly, looking at her through his thick black lashes in an oblique way.

"Yes," she said huskily.

"Whatever was all that noise?" Lucy asked, and got a dry glance.

"Nothing important."

"It sounded as if World War III had just broken out," Lucy said in unashamed probing.

"Did it?" Lee wasn't giving anything away. He took Natasha's elbow between those long, firm fingers. "Can you walk?"

"Of course I can," she said, looking down, her face still very pale. What had happened? Nothing important, Lee had said, but what had that meant? Why had Mike come? What had been said between them? She couldn't ask him the questions she was dying to have answered while Lucy stood there watching them with a satisfied expression.

"Oh, you do make a lovely couple," she said, and Natasha felt the irony of that like a knife between the ribs. She gave Lee a quick, upward glance and found him looking at her with an enigmatic face, his mouth straight, his jawline hard, the gray eyes narrowed and expressionless.

It was all so quick. She had agonized over the decision to accept Lee's offer for so long and then the ceremony was performed almost before she realized it was starting. They were on their way back to the house before Natasha surfaced to realize that, at least for the present, she was Lee's wife and wearing his gold ring on her left hand.

There had been a handful of guests at the ceremony and they were following back to the house in other cars. Lee and Natasha were in the long black car. Lee was driving, his face averted from her. She looked at his powerful hands on the wheel, and her brows met as she suddenly noticed the graze marring the brown skin.

"What have you done to your hand?"

Lee's face was immovable. "Nothing."

"It's grazed." That wasn't all, she realized. There were bruises on the other hand. "What happened?" Natasha watched him anxiously. "It was Mike, wasn't it? What happened?"

She saw a muscular spasm in his hard cheek. His mouth tightened. "He wanted to see you."

"Oh," she said, oddly at a loss. After a pause she asked in a low voice, "Why?"

"Why do you think?" Lee took a corner closely and the tires screeched on the road. She saw people's heads swing around. Lee was driving far too fast. "Slow down," she said nervously. She got a brief, hard look but he slowed down.

"What did Mike say?" she asked that in a hurried way, watching him because she was anxious and puzzled by his manner. Lee was angry. Why? What had Mike said or done to make him angry?

"Does it matter? I sent him away," Lee said, and she had the strangest suspicion that his voice was defiant, his face reckless. "He's gone for good," he said, but it was less of a statement than a harsh challenge to her to deny it.

Natasha was speechless. "You sent him away without giving me the chance to make up my own mind whether I saw him or not? How dared you? What right do you think you have to do that? He came to see me, not you. You should have asked me—"

"What good would it have done? He would only have upset you all over again. You said yourself that it was over, you could never marry him now. He had his chance and he blew it."

"You didn't even give me the option—"

"I did what I thought was best for you," Lee said curtly. He drew up outside the house and turned to look at her, his long body graceful as it swiveled toward her. "Forget Porter. It's time you realized you can never go backward. He closed the door on you, not the other way around. Put him right out of your mind."

"Don't order me around!" Her pallor was lost in an angry flush. Her blue eyes were overbright and gleaming with unshed tears. "I don't know how you could do such a thing! You can't decide for me who I see and who I don't. I'm not a possession of yours and I'm not a child. I'm a woman."

"That's debatable," he said with a tight smile that, to Natasha, had a cruel twist to it.

The other cars were drawing up. Lee got out and came around to help her out. Natasha somehow forced herself to smile, look more like an imitation of a happy bride, but it was a wearing struggle and she wasn't sorry when, after allowing her to drink one glass of champagne, James lightly ordered her back to bed.

The brief excursion had tired her. She fell asleep early that evening but she dreamed a good deal during the night and one of the dreams ran close to nightmare. She woke up from it, sweating, shivering, and the room was pitch black. She started out of the grip of terror and her eyes flew open. Someone moved in the room and she gave a smothered yelp of fear until the bedside lamp came on and she saw Lee's concerned face.

"What in God's name were you shouting about? Nightmare?" He stood beside the bed staring at her fixedly. She had sat up, the covers falling away, and she was so disturbed that she wasn't aware of him as a man, merely as another human being, a reassuring presence after the chilling nightmare.

"I suppose so," she muttered unevenly.

"What were you dreaming about?"

She shook her head, her face confused, searching her memory for whatever had made her so frightened, so upset. It had gone, all of it, the events of the nightmare. Only the feelings remained with her, their spell potent even now, a feeling of being lost and alone.

"Tell me," Lee urged roughly, sitting down on the bed and taking both her cold hands.

"I can't remember."

"Perhaps you don't want to remember," Lee said oddly, watching her face.

"Perhaps I don't," she agreed, forcing a smile that wavered.

"I feel okay now," she said, suddenly aware they were alone and it was nighttime and she was in bed.

Their eyes met. Lee gave her a savagely mocking smile. "You can stop shivering," he said. "You're perfectly safe with me."

"I wasn't shivering," she denied, then at his sarcastic look added quickly, "Well, if I was, it was with cold." Her nightdress was made of fine pink nylon and left her shoulders bare and a great deal of her breasts, the tiny shaped cups suspended from the thin ribbon straps merely supporting her warm white flesh rather than concealing it.

Lee's gray eyes slid down over her and she tried to tug her hands away from his in order to cover herself with the bedclothes. He wouldn't release her, a twisted smile tugging at his mouth.

"Being pregnant suits you," he said. "You're even

lovelier. Your skin has a beautiful smooth texture." He let go of her hands at last but it was to touch her shoulder, his fingertips softly following the contour of it, molding the warm rounded flesh and tracing the path of the shoulderbone beneath it. Natasha sat very still in mute, shy anxiety, her lashes lowered and her heart beating very fast inside her. She didn't quite dare to push his hand away. She could feel him staring at her and she sat tensely, every nerve in her body leaping with awareness.

Lee shifted on the bed and she jumped, her eyes flying to his face. He held their nervous gaze, his face unreadable. When those wandering fingers began to skim down toward the rise of her breasts she instinctively put up a hand to stop him, but he took her wrist and without a word, firmly thrust it aside. She shivered, her eyes averted from him, bitterly aware of the movements of those caressing fingers against her breasts.

"Don't be frightened," Lee whispered huskily. "There's no need to feel guilty because you want me to touch you. You do, don't you?"

She felt a hot confusion inside herself at the question. "No," she said automatically, her voice struggling to sound cold and angry. "I don't want you to."

"Liar," he said, laughter in his voice, but there was something else there, too, an unsteady note, an audible excitement. "Do you think I can't feel it?" He bent forward, breathing unevenly, and she felt his lips brush the side of her throat, sliding coaxingly over her skin, while those dangerously seductive fingers sent shock waves of intense sensual feeling beating along the paths of her nerves.

Natasha's breath caught. She opened her lips to pro-

test but her own reaction was too strong. She felt the
words of rejection freezing on her tongue. Her eyes
closed and her head fell back weakly as his lips teased
over her skin. Her body was melting into total submission and she knew it, but she was helpless to do anything
about it. Her own desire had come leaping up out of her
subconscious, as it had the night they first met. Natasha
had been taught as a child that she should not give in to
temptation, she should resist her own weakness, but
with Lee deliberately weakening her inbuilt defenses like
this she found it impossible to remember why she should
stop him.

His mouth covered her own and she clung to him,
kissing him back without protest or reluctance, her hand
against his neck, feeling the rapid beat of his pulse
under her fingers, her body plastic and yielding in his
hands as desire drowned every attempt at thought. The
heated, restless movements of their bodies became
fevered. She could hear Lee's heart hammering and his
breathing becoming painful, until suddenly he thrust
her away and shot off the bed, standing there, dragging
air into his lungs, his face darkly flushed and his gray
eyes burning on her.

"We can't," he said, his hands clenched at his sides.

Natasha lay there, trembling, still rapt in an erotic intensity which made her incapable of thought.

"James told me it might be dangerous," Lee said.
"He warned me not to sleep with you."

The words sank into her mind and she felt the sexual
turmoil inside her diminishing, a quiver of shame and
self-contempt making her turn her face away from Lee's
watchful stare, crimson staining her face.

"Don't look like that!" Lee started forward, anger in

his eyes. "There's nothing to be ashamed of now, Natasha. We're married. That's all that bothered you, isn't it? Well, we've made it legal, so there's no need to give me that accusing look. Nobody is going to despise you because you give way to the way you feel now. There's no need to feel guilty any more."

"Isn't there?" she asked bitterly, because she realized he didn't understand. "Just because you've put a ring on my finger it doesn't make me your property. It isn't just a question of legal permission. There's far more to it than that."

"You wanted me just now," Lee flung at her, his face and voice filled with icy scorn. "Don't try to deny it. You made it all too obvious."

She felt sick with humiliation. No doubt she had. She couldn't bear to look at him. All the excited intensity she had felt in his arms had gone now.

"It isn't real," she whispered. "Can't you see? I believe it should be an act of love, not an act of lust."

"That wasn't lust," Lee snarled in a dangerous voice. "Don't use words like that."

"What was it then?" Natasha asked unsteadily, her skin ice-cold. "It certainly wasn't love—we aren't in love."

"It was—" He stopped the rapid words and for a moment she heard him breathing irregularly. Then he said with wry emphasis, "It was desire, Natasha, which is something very different. You're a very beautiful woman and I want you. Lust is a cold, bitter emotion. Didn't you know that? Lust is a disguised hatred. Desire is a natural reaction to beauty."

"Wanting something doesn't mean it is right to try to take it," Natasha said in a confused whisper.

"I think you're in a very muddled state of mind, Natasha," Lee said in mocking amusement. "You don't know what you want and you aren't ready to admit it even if you're beginning to see it. If you don't want me to touch you, I won't, but try not to be so obvious about being nervous of me. It makes me want to give you something to be nervous about."

Natasha glanced away, trembling, her pulses racing under her hot skin.

"Perhaps if you could just relax when I'm around we wouldn't have these nasty moments," Lee said, walking to the door. He was wearing a black silk robe. His feet were bare and his movements silent. She watched him through her lashes as he opened the door again. "Do you think you'll sleep now?" he asked quietly.

"Yes, thank you," she said, and he went out, but she lay there in the yellow circle of light shed by the bedside lamp for a long time before she finally switched off the light and turned over to try to sleep.

A few days later Lee asked her suddenly if she had told her parents yet about their marriage. Natasha shook her head. She hadn't yet been able to summon up the courage to write.

"You'll have to tell them sometime."

She sighed. "I know. But when I do they're bound to come up to London to find out what on earth is going on."

He smiled, a lazy charm in his gray eyes. "You little ostrich, sooner or later they have to find out, both about the marriage and the baby. The longer you put it off the more difficult it will be."

"I know."

"Would you like me to drive down there and see

them?'' he offered, and she was tempted to accept but in the end she shook her head, her long dark hair flicking against her cheek.

"It is my responsibility."

He shrugged his wide shoulders, studying her thoughtfully. "Invite them to stay for a few days. I ought to meet them."

"If it was a real marriage..." she began, and Lee's brows jerked together in a savage frown.

"It's real," he snapped. "I've got the wedding certificate to prove it and you're wearing my ring and expecting my baby. How real do you want it?"

Natasha looked at him in dazed surprise, her eyes enormous. "Don't jump down my throat. You know what I mean."

"I don't," Lee told her tersely. "I never know what the hell you mean. I don't think you do, either. Like most women you're a law unto yourself, a mystery, completely incomprehensible. I look at you sometimes and wonder what's going on inside that head of yours. Whatever it is, the result is baffling."

When he stopped biting the fast, angry words out, Natasha took a long breath and said indignantly, "What did I say to get that sort of reaction? You say I'm baffling. What do you think you are?"

He relaxed slightly, giving her a wry, rueful smile, his eyes self-mocking. "Sorry. I'm just a poor misunderstood man, that's all, and sometimes it makes me so mad I could spit teeth."

She laughed. "I think you just did."

"Oh, that was nothing. You should see me when I'm really in a temper."

"No, thank you. I've seen enough of that already," she said.

Lee's smile widened. "Stick with me, baby. You ain't seen nothing yet," he teased.

When he smiled like that she liked him, liked him very much, and she felt a strange little quiver of excitement at the prospect of introducing him to her family as her husband. They had not been exactly bowled over by Mike. They had liked him well enough, but Natasha knew that they were going to be dazed when they met Lee. Especially Linda, she thought, not displeased by the idea of seeing her sister's incredulous face as she met Lee and realized what sort of man her sister had married.

She looked at Lee through her drooping lashes, a pulse beating at her throat. He was very good-looking, she thought. Autumn sunlight gleamed along his cheekbones, giving his brown skin a taut texture that made her suddenly wonder what it felt like. If their marriage had been anything but a matter of convenience she might have touched him to find out, ran her fingertips along the strong line of jaw and cheek, felt the smooth toughness of his skin.

"So you'll write at once?" he was asking, and she watched his mouth with an absorbed fascination, remembering how she had stared at it the night they met, seeing again the explosive sexual promise in the firm warm line of it.

"Are you daydreaming again?" His voice wasn't annoyed this time. It had amusement in it and she looked up reluctantly from her study of his mouth to meet smiling gray eyes.

"Sorry. Yes, I'll write at once. Are you sure you want to have them here?"

"Sure," he said. "I have no parents myself. I was an only child. I'm rather short on family and I'll be happy to meet yours."

"They're very ordinary," she said, and Lee smiled.

"I wasn't expecting you to produce people with three heads."

Natasha laughed. "I meant—"

"I know what you meant." His voice was gentle and she looked into his eyes searchingly.

"I love them very much," she said in faintly shy tones. She realized she wanted him to like them, wanted them to like him. It was important, although she hadn't realized it until now.

He nodded, his face grave. "And they love you?"

"Yes."

"Don't worry," he said, as though he could read her mind. "It will be okay. If they love you they'll understand and forgive you."

When she sat down later to write that letter she wondered if he was right. Would her family understand and forgive? She took hours to put it all down on paper. The bed was covered with screwed up balls of paper by the time she had managed to set it all down in what she felt was an honest way. Of course, she did not go into details or explain the exact course of events. She was more concerned with giving her parents a fairly clear idea of the present situation and the reasons why she had married without waiting for them to be there.

Lee came in later and looked at the discarded, screwed-up sheets of paper, his face wry. "Hard, was it?"

She grimaced, her pink lips moving in a rueful grin. "It wasn't easy."

"But I can post this, can I?" he asked, picking up the envelope and weighing it on his open palm, staring at it.

"Yes," Natasha said. "You can post it." The sooner it was on its way the better. She knew she was already very nervous at the idea that her parents would be reading as much as she had told them. She might withdraw the letter if Lee didn't post it. She was dying to tear it up and let sleeping dogs lie, but that was a cowardly impulse and she was ashamed of herself. "Post it," she said huskily, and Lee looked at her shrewdly then came over and bent and kissed her on the forehead as if she was a child. It was a reassuring, gentle kiss and nothing to get uptight about, so Natasha smiled at him shyly as he turned and walked away.

CHAPTER TEN

JAMES TURNED TO HER, the sunlight gleaming on his blond hair, and asked cheerfully, "Would you like to start getting up for an hour a day?"

She was excited by the suggestion, her face lighting up, and he laughed as he saw her expression. "Yes, please, can I really?"

"If you're very good," he said in that faintly scolding voice that he used when he was acting out his role of doctor. "You can get dressed and sit in a chair downstairs for exactly one hour a day. If there are no signs of any problems we might extend it in a little while."

"Thank you," she said breathlessly, as though he had given her some wonderful present, and James looked amused. He was a kind young man, slightly patronizing at times, and he tended to treat Natasha as though she was more a child than a woman, but she didn't mind that. At this moment she did not mind about anything.

"I'm so sick of lying in bed," she told him, and he nodded.

"I thought you might be."

"It's so boring."

"I can imagine," he agreed. "I wouldn't mind doing a bit of it, myself, though. I rarely get the chance to stay in bed even at night."

"Tragic," Lee mocked, coming into the room and

giving his friend a dry smile. "My heart bleeds for you."

"You unsympathetic swine," James said, grinning. "I work myself to a standstill and that's all the thanks I get. I don't know why I do this job."

"You're a saint," Lee said. "Why not admit it and stop being so modest?"

James moved toward the door, laughing. "Well, if you insist, but you said it first. Remember, Natasha, one hour only and no excitement." He gave Lee a sideways, teasing look. "Of any kind," he added, his mouth crooked.

"Sadist," Lee said, but although he laughed he had a distinct wryness in his face as James went out.

Natasha was aware that her face was rather flushed. The little dig that James had just made had made her feel very uncomfortable and Lee's dry glance at her did not make her any more relaxed. To cover her embarrassment she launched into excited speech.

"Guess what. James said I could get up for an hour a day from now on as long as I sit in a chair and don't do anything."

"That's marvelous," Lee said warmly, smiling at her. "Obviously his rest cure is beginning to work. You have far more color these days."

"I was getting very bored in bed, though. It will be great to be able to come downstairs and feel normal again."

"I never get bored in bed," Lee said, eyeing her through his lashes with a taunting little smile.

She ignored it as much as she could, trying to shut off the instinctive leap of her senses at the mocking invitation in those gray eyes. "Aren't you going to work today?"

"I'm taking a day off," he told her. "That's the great thing about being the boss. There's nobody to tell you what to do and you can please yourself." He stood with his hands in his pockets, watching her. "You ought to try it sometime. Stop being such a scared little rabbit and go after what you want." There was soft amusement in his voice now, but Natasha could see the gleam of his eyes through his lashes and she knew the amusement was a cloak for something else. Lee was trying to taunt her into a reaction she was determined not to give him.

"I want to get up and come downstairs for an hour now," she said, pretending not to understand that hidden taunt.

He shrugged, grinning wryly. "Okay." He brought her dressing gown and pulled back the covers. Natasha swung her legs out of the bed and stood up, swaying slightly at the unaccustomed feel of her feet on the floor. Lee put his arm around her and she felt her lungs compress, her ribs hurting as she inhaled sharply. She averted her face but he was watching her closely and he knew his touch had shaken her.

She slid into her dressing gown and slowly walked toward the door. Her mind was tormented by recognition of the fact that Lee was continually watching her, looking at her, waiting for some sign of weakness that he would immediately take advantage of.

He wanted to force out of her some admission that she refused to give him. Whenever she came close to letting herself realize what it was exactly that Lee wanted out of her she hurriedly stopped thinking, afraid even to name it to herself. She knew she had given him what he wanted the night they met and Lee wanted her to go on giving it, that nameless emotion, that intense sensual response, that Natasha now found so shameful, so painful, about which she felt so horrified.

Guilt ate at her whenever she remembered how she had felt. Lee had angrily said she must not use ugly words for it, but lust was the only word she knew for how she had felt because she had certainly not been in love with him that night. She had been in love with Mike. As she sat down in the deep armchair by the window she felt a queer little shock of realization. She had been in love with Mike. Once. But she wasn't in love with him now. She did not even know when that love had died, only that it had withered gradually over the weeks. There was something bitterly painful about admitting that. Love was like a plant that needs air to survive. Mike's absence had smothered her love for him and that raised the whole question of the reality of love, for if she only loved Mike when he was there to be loved, how real was love itself?

"What on earth are you scowling about now?" Lee asked with a faintly irritated tone, and she looked up at him, her blue eyes wide with startled surprise.

"Was I? Sorry."

"That doesn't answer the question," he muttered. "But then you never do, do you? Answer questions, I mean. You dodge issues more than anyone I ever met. You haven't an ounce of nerve, have you, Natasha?" There was scathing contempt in the question and she flinched from it, frowning, "Oh, you've got a weird sort of personal courage," he went on flatly. "You screw yourself up to face things when you know you must, just as you were ready to go down and tell your parents the truth. But you have to be forced to face things, don't you? You don't do it willingly. In fact, your cowardice is maddening.''

Her cheeks were hot. ''Is it?'' She was hurt and angry but she refused to enter into one of his deliberately set-up arguments. She had a good idea why he was trying to sting her into response, and she wasn't falling for it.

He looked down at her, eyes narrowed, and she had the distinct impression he was searching for some way of taunting her into a more uncontrolled response.

''You've been conditioned,'' he said tersely.

''Have I? I suppose we all have,'' Natasha said lightly. ''In one way or another, particularly women. We grow up having it thrust down our throats that women are this or that and do this or that. Nobody lets you grow up to find out. They start conditioning you in your cradle.''

''We're talking about different things,'' Lee said, his irritated shrug pushing her words away. ''You feel guilty about what happened between us, don't you? That's what is wrong with you. Every time I look at you I see it in your face. You're carrying around a damned great load of guilt as big as a house and you aren't even trying to shed it. You hug it to you as though you love it.''

''I don't love it,'' she said, stung at last, her eyes angry. ''I wish I could forget it.''

''You admit that's how you feel, then,'' Lee said, a bitter satisfaction in his face. ''At least that's something.''

''I haven't ever denied it. I feel guilty, yes. Is that what you have been trying to make me say? All right. I feel guilty, guilty, guilty!'' Her voice had risen so high it was almost piercing, and the words rang around the room and as she heard them she felt sick at the uncontrolled emotion in her own voice. She closed her mouth, swallowing, her eyes shifting away from his face.

"I asked you this once before and I didn't get any satisfactory answer," Lee said, his eyes staring into her face, trying to force her to look back at him. "Do you feel guilty because of Porter? Or because you thought it was wrong to go to bed with me at all?"

"What difference does it make?" she asked wearily.

"A hell of a lot," Lee said tersely. "If you're guilty because of Porter I can understand it, but if you hate yourself for having wanted me we are talking about a totally different situation."

"I don't want to talk about it," Natasha said.

"I know you don't. You've tried to avoid the subject every time I've brought it up."

"Then why can't you leave it alone?" she burst out, trembling.

"I can't, that's why," he said, his eyes fierce. "I've got to know. If it has nothing to do with the way you felt about Porter—"

"Of course it has," she interrupted, because she felt nervously afraid of the end of that sentence, although she didn't quite know why or what it was she was afraid he was going to say. "I loved Mike."

"Yet you never went to bed with him," Lee said rapidly, and the words made her heart miss a beat. Her eyes flickered nervously away from his watchful stare, her brows jerked together in an anxious frown.

Lee waited, staring, and then said, "Did you?" in a low, terse voice.

Natasha kept her eyes averted.

"Why was that, Natasha?" Lee asked, his tone becoming very soft and mocking. "Why didn't you ever let him make love to you? If you were madly in love with him and planning to marry quite soon—"

"I preferred to wait," she said huskily.

Lee laughed and her color deepened. "Very restrained," he said, the taunt only too áudible. "And I bet it didn't cost you a sleepless night, did it? You may have been planning to marry him but you weren't going crazy with frustration because he wasn't making love to you. You were quite ready to wait for that. You weren't in any hurry, were you? It didn't bother you at all."

"I'm not discussing my relationship with Mike with you!" She would have got up and walked away if she hadn't been afraid her legs would give way underneath her. She was trembling as she sat there and her knees felt weak.

"I've got it, though, haven't I? You didn't want Porter that way."

She was furious with him for forcing the discussion on her, and she refused to answer questions like that because they were far too dangerous.

Lee waited until he saw she wasn't going to answer, then he said dryly, "Let's have it out in the open, shall we? You have some crazy notion that love and sex are separate issues, don't you? You told yourself you loved Mike Porter and you were planning to marry him and live with him all your life, yet you weren't sexually attracted to him."

"You have no right to say that! What makes you think you know any such thing?" Natasha was incoherent with anguish.

"The facts speak for themselves. You'd been dating Porter for months, you claimed to be in love with him,

yet you had never let him touch you except to kiss you
now and then. But within a couple of hours of meeting
me we were in bed together. . . ."

She put her hands over her face, hiding the burning
flush covering her from brow to chin, and Lee bent
down and pulled her hands away, his fingers ruthless.

"Don't keep hiding from it. It's the truth, and the
sooner you face it the wiser for you."

"You're twisting it all," she stammered, and he
shook his head, his gray eyes fixing her stare inexorably.

"I wanted you the minute I saw you and you felt the
same way. I'm sure that if you had been strictly sober
you would never have admitted that, even to yourself,
but you were half-drunk and your inhibitions were loos-
ened."

"Don't keep reminding me," she muttered. "Do you
think I'm proud of it?"

"I'm aware you're not," Lee said. "You're as guilty
as hell about it."

"If you know that, why keep prodding away at me?"
she asked him bitterly.

"To get the truth," he told her. "We've got some of
it at last, haven't we? You admit you weren't really in
love with Porter at all."

"I didn't say that!"

"You didn't have to; it was obvious. If you had been
genuinely in love you would have wanted him, and you
didn't." Lee paused and she heard the deep harsh
breath he took. It sounded far too loud in the quiet
room. "You wanted me," he said thickly, and she
shook like a leaf at the hoarse sound of his voice, because by his insistent probing he had finally got at the
truth and Natasha was being forced to admit it to her-

self, which she had not wanted to, which she would have done anything to avoid.

"You're ashamed of it, but you did," Lee said, but she hardly heard him because her whole mind was obsessed with the truth he had just made her face. She was in love with him. She hadn't even known what it was driving her that night. She had looked into his gray eyes and seen the vital sexuality, the masculine invitation, and without even knowing it everything female within her had responded hungrily. It had been an entirely physical response that night. Her blood had told her what her mind was too blind to recognize. Her body had dictated all her actions and she had melted into his arms in sensual submission without caring about how she would feel next day. Ever since, her conscience had been lashing her for allowing her sensual need to have its way, and she had been too guilty over that to realize that that sexual recognition had been an instant visual signal she might otherwise have ignored but that had been the first impulse of a very real attraction.

"You're going to have to face it one day," Lee said in a quiet voice, watching her.

She had no intention of letting him see that she had.

"Stop feeling guilty and stop hating me," Lee said.

"I don't hate you," she whispered, and she felt him move toward her only to stop short as the phone rang, making them both jump.

Lee said something explosive under his breath. Lucy was out shopping. He turned and walked toward the door. She heard him pick up the phone. The intrusive shrill sound stopped. "Hello? Oh, Lara," he said, and Natasha shut her eyes on a fierce stab of agony. She had forgotten Lara Brennan. She had forgotten all the other women who had trooped through his life. He might be the first man she had ever felt like this about, but she knew that Lee's experience of sexual pleasure was far wider. It didn't mean the same thing to him. He saw it all very differently.

He was laughing at something. "That's great, darling," he said, and Natasha bit her lip.

She had learned quite a bit about the sophisticated attitude to sex while she was working in the advertising agency. She had watched with cool distaste as Nigel ran through pretty girls as though they were disposable hankies. Girls like Sonia Warren took it all in their stride, enjoying the sexual freedom as much as the men did, but Natasha couldn't look at it like that. That was why she had felt so guilty over Lee. Going to bed with him had been a traumatic shock for her conscience. She despised herself for having done it. Even now that she realized she was in love with him she couldn't excuse herself, because she knew Lee was not in love with her. He wanted her. He had said so frankly, and even if he hadn't she would have known by the way he looked at her, the open desire in those gray eyes whenever they were alone.

But Lee had wanted other women and had them and forgotten them. Natasha refused to let him add her to his little list. He might accept the attitude to sex that was the gospel of the consumer society, but Natasha couldn't. It set too low a value on a human being, on emotion, on life itself. Natasha could not face being equated with some sort of instant pleasure, a human equivalent of the frozen meal that could be ready to eat in a quarter of an hour, that was plastic, unreal, briefly satisfying but forgotten an hour later.

That was not what she wanted out of life. She already felt guilty and self-contemptuous. It would get worse if she let Lee seduce her into responding to him again.

She heard the front door open and close. Lucy's voice chimed in the hall. Lee put down the phone and Natasha heard Lucy chattering to him about the price of oranges. Lee sounded curt and indifferent but Lucy didn't seem to notice. She came into the room and looked at Natasha in disbelief. "What are you doing out of bed? You naughty girl—"

"James said I could get up for an hour a day," Natasha said lightly, smiling at her.

"That sounds as if you're improving," Lucy said, openly delighted. "That *is* good news."

"I've got to go out," Lee said to her, his eyes flashing across the room toward her with narrowed concentration. "I'll be back this afternoon. Shall I help you back to bed now? You've been up almost an hour."

"Yes, we don't want to overdo it at first, do we?" Lucy agreed, bustling over to help her up out of the chair. "You get off, Lee, if you're going out. I'll give Natasha a hand upstairs."

He hesitated, then nodded and went out. Natasha heard his car engine race and then the squeal of the tires as he drove away at top speed.

"Come on, poppet," Lucy said, an arm around her waist. As they shuffled through the hall the doorbell went and Lucy clucked her tongue irritably. "Now, who can that be?" She sat Natasha down on the chair in the hall. "Sit still while I see who it is," she said, going to the door.

Natasha stared at the carpet, her head bent, watching

the widening shaft of autumn sunlight as the door opened.

"Yes?" Lucy asked to whoever was ringing, and Natasha's head swung around as she recognized the answering voice.

"I would like to see—" The voice stopped as Natasha stood up, gripping the back of the chair to support herself.

Lucy looked around in surprise at her, taking in her pale, stunned expression. Natasha stared past her at Mike Porter, her mind too dazed to think clearly. He moved and Lucy fell back instinctively to let him walk into the house. Natasha could not have said a word to save her life.

"Hello, Natasha," Mike said in a rough, husky voice, looking at her with shifting, embarrassed eyes.

"I've got to talk to you," Mike said, glancing at Lucy as he spoke.

"She was just on her way back to bed," Lucy pointed out, the merest suspicion of hostility in her voice, as though she picked up the tension between them and was alert for trouble.

"This won't take a minute," Mike said, looking back at Natasha, his eyes pleading with her to agree.

She stood up shakily. "Okay," she said, walking back into the sitting room with Lucy crossly following.

"I don't think—" Lucy began.

Natasha said quietly, "We won't talk for long, Lucy. I promise."

Lucy stared at her, lips folded together in disapproval, then nodded. "If you say so." She hesitated. Natasha said, "We'll call you when Mike is leaving."

Lucy made a snorting little noise and marched out, closing the door behind her with a snap.

Natasha sat down, gesturing. "Sit down, Mike."

He looked around vaguely and chose a chair that he moved slightly so that it was close to her. Natasha watched him with an odd sense of incredulity. It was strange to see him again. It was only a matter of a few months since they last met yet in that space of time so much had happened.

He looked exactly the same and yet he looked different, but the difference was in her, not in Mike. It was in the way she saw him, the angle of vision that was contrasting how she had once felt with how she felt now. His brown hair, warm brown eyes, healthy fresh coloring, were all the same. He was wearing a rough tweed sports jacket and a pair of dark brown pants. He sat down with his hands on his knees and looked at her, meeting her eyes with an uneasy, nervous smile.

"How are you?"

"Okay," she said, although she did not feel okay at this moment. She felt very odd indeed. She felt like someone at the wrong end of a kaleidoscope.

"I've tried to see you several times," he said, glancing at the door, his face morose. "Farrell wouldn't let me."

She looked down, trying to keep expression off her face.

"I rang and called," Mike said. "I didn't get anywhere. And you didn't answer any of my letters."

"Letters?" Natasha looked up, startled.

Mike's mouth twisted. "He didn't show them to you, I suppose? I had a suspicion he wouldn't."

Natasha was very stiff in her chair. Lee had suppressed letters from Mike? How dare he? She was burning with indignation at the realization. How could he do such a thing? Did he think he was her owner?

"I've been hanging around in the shop along the road," Mike said, and she looked at him incredulously. He made a wry face. "They were a bit nasty at first until I hinted I was a private detective watching someone and then they were so eager to know what was going on that they didn't try to chuck me out of the shop."

"Why were you hanging around there?" Natasha asked, her face full of uneasy curiosity.

"I had to see you and I waited until Farrell went out," Mike said.

"Oh," Natasha said. He had shot over here the moment he saw Lee drive away, obviously. "Why did you have to see me?" she asked. "Mike, there isn't any point, don't you see that?"

"I had to," Mike said roughly. "You see, I wrote to my brother and told him what you'd said about my mother."

Natasha's eyes rounded; she drew a quick breath.

Mike looked at her with grim misery. "Kenneth isn't a great letter writer. He didn't reply at once. When he did I had to read it three times before I could believe my eyes." He put his hands in his hair, ruffling it violently in a gesture she had seen him make before. "You can guess what he said," he muttered. "You were right about his wife, about why Ken stays in Australia. I was shaken rigid. I dashed around to see you and of course your flat had been taken over by someone else. That shook me again. I went to your office and Herries told me you were getting married. I'd have come around then and there but I had to think. I went back home and I—" He broke off, swallowing. "I had words with my mother."

Natasha watched him, her face compassionate. "I'm sorry," she said gently. That must have been hard for him. It wasn't just in her that the difference lay, after all. Mike was different. His face was older, tougher, more assertive. She could see it now.

"We had a very nasty scene," Mike said, tight-lipped. "She cried at first, then she got annoyed, but finally—" He broke off, passing his hand over his face as though to erase the memory. "Well, I know now that you weren't imagining anything. I'm sorry, Natasha. I really loused things up between us, didn't I?"

"You aren't to blame," she said. "You believed her because she was your mother, after all. I realized that. It was natural."

He laughed bitterly. "It never entered my head that she might be trying to break us up. I must be stupid, blind. I didn't even think of it." He looked at her pleadingly. "I must have hurt you pretty badly. I had to come around and see you, try to apologize."

She smiled. "That was nice of you."

"I came before, on your wedding day," Mike said, his scowl returning.

Natasha remembered it vividly. So that was why he had come? Had he told Lee as much?

"I knew I had to see you before it was too late," Mike said. "I wanted to ask you to give me another chance. It was all my fault we quarreled that day, my fault you met Farrell. I was going to ask you to marry me instead of him, but he wouldn't let me see you. He chucked me out bodily. I was so livid I walked to cool down, meaning to come back when I felt I could face him again without going for his jugular, but when I got back there was no reply and then I realized I was really too late."

She nodded gravely. "We left to get married just after you and Lee had the row."

Mike looked at her sharply. "You heard it? You knew I was there?"

Natasha nodded.

"And you didn't want to see me," Mike said slowly. "He was right, then."

"Right?" Her question came out in a terse voice. What had Lee said to him?

She heard the sound of tires screeching on the road outside, then a car door slammed and there were running feet on the pavement. Mike sat up in his chair, looking toward the door with an apprehensive, aggressive face, a mixed expression that might have been comical if Natasha had been in a humorous mood, but in her state of nervous tension she found nothing funny in Mike's bristling alarm.

Lee came into the room like an express train, his long-limbed body vibrating with temper, his eyes murderous.

Mike got out of his chair to confront him, hunched in a fighting stance, but as Lee looked at him, his lip curling back in a furious snarl, Natasha said icily, "How dared you keep back letters addressed to me? And refuse to let Mike speak to me? How dared you?"

Lee didn't take his eyes off Mike. The set of his body had danger written all over it.

"He had done you nothing but harm," he said through his teeth. "What would have happened if I'd let him see you that morning? He'd have upset you all over again, but you would still have married me, so it would all have been for nothing. He would just have given you more heartache. I wasn't letting him near you."

She began to speak angrily and he whirled, fixing her

with darkened gray eyes that shot warning at her. "Don't make me lose my temper, Natasha, because I'm in no mood for that right now, although I'm a patient man generally."

"Patient," she gasped, raging. "You?"

"Just shut up and let me deal with it," Lee said curtly. He looked back at Mike. "If you have any decency you'll clear out and never come back. It's over. She's mine. You had your chance and you blew it, and in this world you never get another one."

Mike stared into Lee's narrowed eyes for a moment, his face full of shifting, conflicting feelings, then he slowly walked out of the room. Natasha heard the front door close behind him.

Lee's shoulders slowly relaxed, the tension draining out of him. He turned, a hand at his tie, loosening it. Natasha looked at him angrily.

"How could you do a thing like that? I had a right to see those letters and make up my own mind about what to do about Mike. Why did you do it?"

"I've told you why," Lee informed her coolly. "I did it in your own interests."

"My interests?" Her voice was scathing.

"I knew you wouldn't be happy with him," Lee said.

"How could you know a thing like that? How dared you dictate my life to me like that?"

"You didn't love him—you never had, you just thought you did," Lee said as calmly as though they were discussing the weather.

She was breathless with outrage. "Oh, you know better than I do what I feel, do you? I'm not allowed to know what I want, what I think. You know my feelings better than I do."

"Yes," he said, running one hand over his thick black hair, a sudden wry smile twisting his mouth. "Oh, yes, Natasha, I do."

She was suddenly very nervous. Her heart stopped beating for one flash of time, her breathing thickened and became unsteady. She couldn't meet the mocking gray eyes and had to look away. Her lips parted but not a sound issued from them. Natasha swallowed, trembling.

"And when you're ready to admit how you feel we'll discuss it again," Lee said dryly, walking out of the room.

CHAPTER ELEVEN

SHE WAS HALF-ASLEEP in the bed a few days later when Lee walked into the room and pulled back the curtains, letting a pale gray flood of winter daylight fall across her flushed face. She blinked, starting to sit up, then fell back, looking at him in nervous surprise. He came over and put a cup of tea on the bedside table.

"Sleep well?"

"Yes, thank you," she said warily, eyeing him with a frown between her brows.

"There's a letter for you," he said, holding out an envelope, and Natasha stared at it without taking it for a few seconds, a tremor of pain running through her.

"From your parents," Lee said unnecessarily, since she had already realized why he had brought it in here. He had recognized the postmark. Natasha had already recognized her father's handwriting.

Lee's face had an understanding, rueful smile. "Open it and get it over with," he said gently.

She sat up and took the envelope. Her fingers trembled as she tore it open, the stiff blue paper ripping as she clumsily extracted the letter.

She read it very quickly, her lower lip unsteady, while Lee watched her pale face. Tears stung her eyelashes. She held the letter out to him and he regarded her quizzically.

"Read it," she said in a husky voice.

He took it and read it, then looked at her, his mouth tender. "It's a very nice letter," he said. "Congratulations."

Natasha's blue eyes widened and her pale skin stretched around them as her bewilderment deepened. "Congratulations? What does that mean?" she demanded half indignantly.

"On having parents like that," Lee said. "I had an idea you did."

"Did you?" Her puzzled annoyance subsided. "Why?"

"You had to come from somewhere," he said enigmatically.

Natasha half smiled. "I suppose everybody does, but that doesn't explain—"

"You always want things in black and white," Lee said wryly. "Half tones are often more true to life." He looked at the cup on the bedside table. "Drink your tea while it's hot."

It was lukewarm but she drank it, eyeing him over the rim of the cup through her lashes.

"I'll tell Lucy they will be here next weekend, then," he said. "I gather Linda is your sister?"

She nodded. "It doesn't mention Jack, so I suppose it will just be my parents and Linda who will be coming." Her stomach churned at the thought of facing them all and the pallor of her skin deepened again.

Lee put his hand on top of hers, his skin warm and comforting as it rested on her own. "Don't worry so much. It will be okay."

"How can you say that?" she asked, brushing a hand across her wet eyes. "You don't know them. They'll be

disappointed in me. I didn't expect they would be angry.
I knew it would make them sad.''

"It's a kind and loving letter," Lee said, forehead
creased in a frown.

"Of course it is. I didn't expect anything else,"
Natasha flared in nervous irritation. "I knew how they
would feel.''

"Natasha, isn't it time you faced the fact that you're
human, and human beings aren't perfect. We're all
flawed, we all make mistakes and get ourselves into a
muddle sometimes. You have too high a standard for
yourself, for everyone around you. You're too thin-
skinned and sensitive. You worry too much and take life
too seriously." Lee moved closer, looking at her intently. "You have a sort of desperation, at times, that worries me. James put his finger on it when he said you had
an instability.''

She laughed angrily. "Are you saying you think I'm
off my head?''

"Of course not," Lee said, mouth wry. "You're like
a nervous thoroughbred. You can screw up your courage to take high fences but it eats you up. Relax, slow
down. Don't meet life as if it was a fight to the death.''

She looked at him uncertainly. "I didn't know I did.''

"Oh, yes," he said, smiling at her. "You're highly
strung and delicate. That's why you're sitting in that
bed, why you're going to have to stay there for a long
time. Calm down.''

"I'll try," she said, and he touched her cheek with
one long forefinger, the light trail on her skin making
her quiver and look away with flickering uncertainty.
Lee stood up, his hand dropping away.

"I must get off to work now. I have a lot of business

to get through today." He pushed back a strand of thick black hair from his forehead in an impatient gesture. "I may be back late. Don't lie there fretting all day."

"No, sir," she said, smiling at his slightly autocratic tone.

He eyed her humorously. "And don't be saucy."

Natasha laughed. "I just can't please you, can I?"

"Oh, I think you could," he murmured mockingly, looking at her sideways as he turned away. "If you really tried...."

He walked out before she could think of anything to say in answer to that deliberate tease and her skin ran with heated color as his words sank home. Her pulses were flickering like the lights on a Christmas tree, a bright unsteady glow inside her.

She hurriedly looked at the sky. Winter was falling over the city like a dull gray blanket, closing in the streets, the chill of the air leaving swirls of frost on the windows first thing in the morning. She could remember days like this in Dorset when the stripped trees had a stark beauty on such a pale sky, and the soft drifting mists clung to the edges of fields, lending distanced to familiar views.

She was afraid. Afraid to commit herself to Lee when she had a conviction that he would not commit himself to her, afraid that the way she felt now was as unreal as her other brief, unhappy excursions into love, afraid of life itself when she tried to look ahead into a shuttered future as veiled as those misty winter fields at home.

The only time she had ever taken a wild gamble with life, she thought, was the night she met Lee, and look where that had got her! Being alive was as dangerous as Russian roulette. Each action you took was like pointing a loaded pistol at your head. The safest thing was to do nothing, feel nothing, risk nothing, but then that wasn't living at all. You were just walling yourself up if you took no risks.

Lucy came bustling into the room a few minutes later with her breakfast tray and news of what was happening in the big world outside. Natasha listened as she ate her cornflakes and her boiled egg and toast. Lucy did not require any answers. All she wanted was an ear. Lucy was a communicator, a walking radio.

"Good girl," she said approvingly as she took the tray. "You're eating much better." When she smiled, Lucy had a kind, soft face and Natasha smiled back at her. There was something soothing about Lucy's nannylike approval. If only you could please everyone as easily, Natasha thought. Wasn't that what everyone wanted? Approval? It was rarely so easy to achieve.

That afternoon she was sitting by the window with one eye on the paperback she was reading and the other on the constant stream of traffic passing along the street outside, when Lee's car swerved into the curb. Natasha felt her heart halt and pick up. She knew she was coloring. He had said he was going to be late tonight. Had he got through his business earlier than he had expected?

Then she saw the girl getting out of the passenger seat and her breath caught in a stab of pain. Lee stood on the pavement, his face in profile, talking to Lara Brennan as she joined him. They turned and walked toward the house and Natasha looked back down at her book with blind eyes.

She heard their voices in the hall a moment later, then the door into the sitting room was pushed open and Lee walked in with the girl at his side.

Natasha looked up at them steadily, masking the emotions eating her, and Lee said, "Natasha, you haven't met Lara, have you? Lara, my wife, Natasha."

Lara Brennan came over with her hand extended, smiling. Natasha automatically shook hands, somehow smiling back. It was an effort and she knew it was a stiff, artificial smile that did not reach her eyes. Lee was watching her, his face unreadable.

"I'll just run up and get the score," Lee said, turning on his heel and vanishing.

Lara looked down at Natasha with quizzical eyes. "We popped in to pick up some music sheets. I'm off to the States tomorrow to do a tour and Lee was running through the stuff I'm taking with me."

"I see," Natasha said stiltedly.

Lara was wearing an elegant olive-green suit that had a black silk scarf knotted between the lapels. She looked casual, smart, confident, and Natasha knew she could never compete with her. Lara had a vitality that came over even when she wasn't talking or moving. Energy and humor sparked in her eyes and her figure was warm and compelling, and, no doubt, irresistible to the opposite sex.

"I've been dying to meet the mystery girl," Lara said, laughing, pulling up a chair and sitting down. "We almost met that day you fainted, but you wouldn't remember that. I was in the taxi with Lee. He was in quite a state when he saw you tumble over like that."

Natasha smiled, her face blank, the movement of her mouth forced.

"When's the baby due?" Lara asked frankly. "It hardly shows yet, does it?"

"No," Natasha admitted slowly. "Next March," she

added in a tight little voice. How much did Lara know about the situation? Had Lee told her everything? That made Natasha feel ill. She couldn't meet Lara's direct gaze.

"I'm dying to have one," Lara said, and Natasha's head lifted on a sharp, indrawn breath, her eyes flying to Lara's face as if to check she had heard correctly. Lara was smiling, her face wistful.

"Don won't hear of it yet, though. He says I ought to get myself established in the business first. If you lose a whole year your career goes off the boil and you may never catch up."

Natasha had her eyes fixed on the other girl's face, bewilderment and intent absorption in her stare. "Don?" she repeated. Who was Lara talking about?

"My husband," Lara said.

Natasha's nerves jerked as if at the touch of fire. "Your husband?"

"Don Grafton," Lara expanded. "The composer." She laughed. "He wrote 'Fairground', my big hit. You know?"

"Yes, I know it, of course," Natasha said huskily. "It's very good."

"I like it," Lara agreed, smiling.

Natasha couldn't take her eyes off her. "I didn't know you were married," she said, wondering how long they had been married and what Don Grafton thought of Lara's relationship with Lee.

"Oh, we got hitched six months ago," Lara said cheerfully. "We stayed here with Lee while our own flat was being done up. Don and Lee were working together on the score for a musical. I expect he told you about it. It was very handy for us to be under the same roof for a few weeks. Don and Lee could get together more often. Don was getting a bit fraught because he could never get Lee tied down long enough to do any real work. You know Lee. He's always on the move. He's very busy—of course, Don knew that, but actually sharing the place with him for a while gave them a chance to get down to it."

Natasha was dazed. "Lee worked on a musical score with your husband?"

"Yes," Lara said, looking at her oddly. "Didn't he tell you? He's a funny one. He does like to play his cards close to his chest, doesn't he?"

"What sort of music? What did Lee do?"

"He was working on the book," Lara said, then caught her eye and grinned. "The words. Lee wrote the dialogue, the lyrics and so on. It is a musical version of *Pride and Prejudice.*"

Natasha could only stare. "And Lee wrote the words?"

"Hardly," said Lee's voice coolly from the door and Natasha flicked a rapid glance toward him. "Jane Austen did that. I just lifted her dialogue wherever I could. Even the songs used a lot of her actual words."

"Is it going to be put on?" Natasha asked, and Lara laughed.

"They're keeping their fingers crossed."

"That's a moot point," Lee said almost at the same time, his face rueful. "Maybe one day it will be," he went on, shrugging. He held out a great sheaf of music sheets and Lara took them, hugging them to her with fervor.

"Thanks. You approve?"

"I've made a list of the stuff I don't want you to use," Lee said. "Not your image."

Lara made a face. "I'm going if you're going to start talking about that," she said lightly. She gave Natasha a smile. "Nice to meet you. We should have done it sooner. Now I'm off to the States and God knows when I'll get back. Good luck with the baby and if I'm back in time for the christening, you'll ask me along, won't you?"

"Yes, of course," Natasha said brightly. "It was nice to meet you, too. I hope your tour is successful."

"So do I," Lara said with a groan as she went toward the door. "Bye, see you again sometime, I hope."

Lee stood there, looking narrowly at Natasha. "I'm still going to be back late," he said. "I've got to drive Lara home now."

She nodded, not quite meeting his eyes, and he waited a moment and then went out without adding anything.

That evening she was reading in bed, the room lighted only softly by the bedside lamp, when Lee tapped at the door and strolled in, glancing at her. "Had a good day?" he asked, and she nodded.

"Have you?"

Usually he just shrugged but tonight he came over and sat on the bed, yawning slightly, beginning to tell her about his job, talking about some studio work he had been supervising and a new group he had just signed up. Natasha listened, sensing that he was in a mood to talk without caring who it was he was talking to. There were lines of weariness around eyes and mouth, a tired droop to his shoulders.

He halted, grimacing at her. "Sorry to bore you."

"You didn't. I was fascinated."

"Were you?" He gave her a rueful smile. "Nice of you to say so, but shoptalk is only ever fascinating for insiders, isn't it? I try not to start talking about the job to people." He moved to stand up.

"Why didn't you tell me that Lara was married?" Natasha asked, and he stiffened, shooting her a wary look.

"Didn't I?"

"You know you didn't."

Their eyes met and Lee made a wry little face. "I suppose I just forgot." Then he gave her a mocking smile. "Maybe I forgot deliberately. Maybe I thought it was a good idea that you should think I was involved elsewhere."

"Why?" She asked the question in a flat voice. She had been wondering all day about it, asking herself why Lee had deliberately given her the wrong impression.

Lee did not answer, but his face had a self-derision he didn't try to hide, his mouth crooked, his eyes angry.

"Why?" she repeated, staring at him.

He shifted in an uneasy way, pushing back his hair with restless fingers. "Does it matter?"

"Of course it matters," Natasha broke out. "Lara said you liked to play your cards close to your chest and she was right, wasn't she? You're always doing things, saying things, without explaining why. Why did you think you had the right to choose for me whether I should see Mike or not? Why did you let me think you were having an affair with Lara? I don't like having my life arranged for me as if I was a child."

"You'll just have to get used to it," Lee muttered.

"What?" Her face had become flushed with anger and her blue eyes were flashing as she stared at him.

His jaw had an aggressive tilt to it. "You aren't fit to be let out on your own," he told her. "Somebody has to take charge of you before you entirely wreck your life.''

"Take charge—" She was almost speechless, her voice husky and stifled with rage. "You're not taking charge of me. I'm not a half-wit.''

"You behave like one. Look at the night we met," he said, bristling. "Do you call that sane behavior?''

"Don't sidetrack me," Natasha said, looking away. "That doesn't explain why you let me think you were having an affair with Lara.''

"Lara and I did have a few dates at one time," he said. "When she first started working for us, but when she met Don it altered everything.''

"Then why let me think what I did?''

"It helped.''

"Helped? Who?''

"Me," Lee said tersely. "It helped me. It saved my face, if you must have it. That may not mean much to you, but I'm a man and it means a lot to me.''

She stared, not understanding. "Why did it save your face?''

He groaned, his mouth twisting. "Are you stupid?''

"Yes," she said, and he gave a short laugh.

"Well, you said it." He shot her a brief look from under his lashes and dark color crawled into his cheeks. "I needed some sort of protection," he said enigmatically.

"And Lara was it?" Natasha wished she knew what it was he was trying to get across to her because whatever it was he was making a bad job of it. She didn't have a clue. Hesitantly she asked, "Were you afraid I might try to trap you? Is that it? You thought I might blackmail you if I didn't think you were involved with anyone else?''

The gray eyes looked at her with grim humor. "My God, I sometimes think I must be crazy," he said inexplicably. "What is there behind those big blue eyes? Air?"

She glared at him. "I'm no good at guessing other people's motives. I can't do crosswords, either."

Lee looked at her again, a strange restless uncertainty in his face, then he moved, his hands closing around her shoulders, lifting her toward him like a doll. "Then I'll give you a clue," he muttered as he bent his head.

Natasha angrily struggled, twisting her head away. Did he really think he could handle her as he pleased, when he pleased? He was just evading the question, refusing to discuss his earlier deception, trying to change the subject again to one he preferred, only this time he wasn't getting away with it. She heard Lee take a harsh breath, then his fingers seized her chin and held it, so that she could not break away without hurting herself.

She flickered a nervous look at him and saw his face darkened by temper, a cruelty in the hard line of his mouth. Trembling, she whispered, "Don't, Lee." She was afraid of him when he looked like that. The masculine violence leaped out at her from those cold gray eyes.

"It's time you faced it, Natasha," he grated. "You can't keep running away from yourself or life. It always catches up with you in the end. If I have to keep you locked up for a hundred years I'll make you admit it."

"Admit what?" she asked, her skin ice-cold with shock.

"This," he said, and took her mouth with a ruthless drive for response that shot away all her defenses and made her body pulse with electric heat, the hungry clamor of her own passion meeting his and intensifying his demand. Her hands stole slowly around his neck, her body slackened and leaned against him, yielding in feminine weakness to the fierce pressure of his embrace. As she surrendered to her own need the drowning sensuality she had known the night they met took over and she groaned, her body shivering, restless, aroused.

He framed her face between his hands and looked into her drowsy eyes a moment later. "The night we met I fell in love when I heard you laughing," he said huskily. "I looked around and there you were and you were so lovely I couldn't take my eyes off you. I had the feeling you were looking at me in exactly the same way."

She had been. She remembered it clearly, standing there, staring at him with absorbed intensity, thinking that he was the most attractive man she had ever seen in her life.

"That night was sheer magic," he said, a tormented look in his eyes. "I was walking on air. You said it yourself—we were in a bubble floating up in the sky. Well, next morning you burst the bubble and I crashed to earth with a vengeance."

"I'm sorry," she whispered, touching his cheek gently. "I behaved very badly."

"You did," he said, looking into her eyes. "I hated you for at least three days, then I started feeling like someone who has been into the Garden of Eden and then got chucked out. I couldn't stop thinking about you. When Porter came around and I jumped to the conclusion that he was trying to blackmail me I could have killed him, not just because I was furious but because I was so jealous of him. I looked at him and I could have throttled him there and then. I was as mad as fire with you, too, because I thought you were in it with him, that I'd been set up. Oh, I was slightly off my rocker by then. It was stupid of me. I knew you, I should have known you would never be involved in anything like that, but at the time I was too angry to stop and think about it."

She was staring at him, her eyes enormous and feverish, a crazy happiness circulating in her veins because he had said he loved her, he had said he had fallen in love that night. The words kept beating in her head and she was dying to ask him if he meant them, because if he did it altered everything, it made the whole world turn on a new axis.

"When I realized how wrong I was and calmed down, I realized I'd got another chance to get back into Eden," Lee said wryly. "But you were pigheaded, you wouldn't let me do what I was dying to do, you refused even to discuss marrying me and I saw my chance slipping away again." He gave a long sigh. "So I had to play a waiting game. I tried to do a little patient infiltrating. I persuaded you to see me now and then, I tried to get to know you, hoping you'd get over Porter and start seeing me as the world's best thing since sliced bread."

She laughed, her eyes bright. "It never occurred to you to come straight out with it and ask me?"

He looked directly into her smiling eyes. "And if I had? What would you have said?"

She considered, her mouth quizzical. "I suppose I would have found it hard to believe at the time and—"

"And you were still in love with Porter, or thought you were," he finished for her. "I began to realize you never had been, though. I started to think and to see that if you had been you would never have rushed into bed with me like that. That was when I really began to hope.''

"Oh, was it?" she asked, piqued.

He looked at her mockingly. "It was the only logical answer," he told her. "Not that I expected logic from you. You are one of the most emotional women I've ever met. Your mind doesn't think. It moves in its own mysterious way. God help the poor male who tries to follow it because he is only going to end up with a violent headache."

"Thank you," Natasha said with dignity.

"But I love you," Lee said. His voice deepened and thickened and he buried his face in the side of her throat, kissing her skin passionately. "I love you, darling, I need you, crazy though you are. I need to look after you and as sure as God made little apples you need me to stop you doing any more crazy things."

Her fingers wove into his thick, vital hair, her breath quickening at the feel of his mouth against her skin.

"And Lara?" she asked unsteadily, and heard him laugh before he lifted his heated face.

"Oh, Lara," he said wryly. "Well, I used her as some sort of shield, I'm afraid. I didn't want you to know you had me on my knees. Lara was my protection, the way I kept you off the scent. Don's my best friend, but, believe me, he is not the guy to stand still for having his wife play games with another man. There hasn't been a thing between me and Lara since she met Don, and although we did date once it was never serious. We're fond of each other but that's all."

Natasha was looking dreamily at him, her eyes half-closed, all her attention given to the sensual promise of his mouth, waiting for the moment when she would feel the touch of it again.

"Are you ready to admit it yet?" Lee asked unsteadily, mocking in his voice but a roughness, too, that spoke of deep emotion, and she looked up into his gray eyes, her lashes fluttering rapidly as she met that intense stare.

She nodded, her mouth dry, unable to say a syllable, her whole body filling with a sensual feeling she need no longer suppress.

"I want to hear you say it," Lee said, his mouth curling at the edges in a mocking little smile. He paused, his face restless. "I need to hear you say it," he added. "I've waited so long and you've kept me in suspense long enough."

"I love you," she whispered. "You're right. I was never in love with Mike. We wouldn't have been right for each other. I never once wanted him the way I—" She cut the sentence off, blushing, and Lee laughed huskily.

"Shameless," he said. "The way you wanted me?" The question was asked very lightly, but there was eagerness in the gray eyes and Natasha made herself throw away the last lingering vestige of shame and guilt, putting her arms around his neck and looking at him with yielding passion.

"Yes, the minute I saw you. It never entered my head for a long time that I was in love with you, but I was, of course. I didn't believe love could come like that. I was ashamed of feeling the way I did about you. I thought love was calm and gentle—"

"And sensible," Lee mocked with tenderness in his eyes.

She laughed. "I suppose so. It was how I was brought up to see it. My parents drummed it into my head that love meant choosing a nice man, getting married, having children and building up a good life together. They never told me that love was like an express train that could knock you down before you knew what had hit you. I wasn't expecting love that night. How could I? I thought I was in love with Mike."

"Champagne is wonderful stuff," Lee said, his eyes glinting at her with laughter in their depths.

She laughed, too. "It was the champagne that wiped out of my head everything I'd grown up believing. Sheer natural instinct made me go off with you like that. I knew it was what I wanted to do, so I did it, but of course next morning I came out of it and all my inhibitions were back with me and I was horrified at what I'd done."

"It showed," Lee said.

"I'm sorry," she murmured, brushing a light kiss across his mouth. "I was mixed up."

"You can say that again." Lee took another kiss, his mouth lingering. "Your mind gave me a lot of heartache."

"My mind was confused," she admitted. "It couldn't understand what was going on. I was feeling more and more disturbed as I faced what I wanted. One part of me kept insisting that the desire I felt was wrong and the other part refused to believe it, didn't want to listen. I was jealous of Lara—"

"Ah," he said, his eyes flaring with satisfaction, and she paused to look at him with wry amusement.

"Oh, you like that, don't you?"

"Yes," he mocked, his mouth amused.

"I'm not sure it was wise of you," Natasha said seriously. "To make me think you had a lot of other women. It reinforced what my parents had taught me—that men and women were different where love was concerned."

Lee frowned. "You'd got it firmly fixed in your head that sex was something shameful, hadn't you?"

"Not exactly that," she denied. "But I did think it was shameful that I should take one look at you and want to go to bed with you."

His frown dissolved in laughter. "Poor Natasha," he murmured, his voice husky.

"If I was inhibited it wasn't my fault. Men are to blame for that."

"Oh, of course, I might have known it would turn out to be my fault in the end somehow," he said dryly.

"Not you personally, but men in general," Natasha insisted. "Men have organized the world for their own convenience for years. They made the laws, moral and otherwise, and it was men who sold women the idea that sexual desire is okay for a man but shameful for a woman."

"I think you'll find that particular male theory has been blown to smithereens lately," Lee said with a look of teasing amusement. "Your trouble is you're old-fashioned."

"I had an old-fashioned upbringing," she admitted. "And the way we met, the fact that you seemed to behave like that all the time, made me feel ashamed and guilty. I knew I would never again be able to jump into bed with a man on sight. I thought you probably did it all the time with every pretty girl you fancied. Don't you see? You seemed to prove what I'd been taught, that desire was what a man felt, while a woman felt nothing but a warm romantic glow.''

Lee started to laugh. ''Wasn't that a narrow interpretation of love? You can't confine love inside one set of reactions or another. Just as every single human being who has ever been born has had a totally unique set of fingerprints, so they've had a unique approach to love. Love is what we want it to be, what we need. It doesn't have any rules. There's no such thing as law or morals where love is concerned. It is just a question of feeling, of real emotion, of caring for one person rather than another, of needing one person rather than another.''

Natasha began to speak and stopped dead, her face stiffening. She felt her whole being jerk to attention. Lee looked at her in alarm and questioning.

''What is it? Are you ill?''

She started to smile, her face full of dawning happiness. Taking his hand she laid it on the swell of her body and Lee felt it, too, under his palm, the tiny fluttering of life inside her.

''It's kicking,'' Lee said in a voice so full of surprise it made her laugh.

''It's the first time I've felt it,'' she said, and knew that her whole feeling about the baby had altered, too. There was no longer any need for guilt or shame. The desire that she had not recognized for love had driven out all feeling but itself, and the life within her was the miracle of love.

Harlequin $\boxed{\textit{Plus}}$

A WORD ABOUT THE AUTHOR

Since she began writing for Harlequin Presents in late
1978, Charlotte Lamb has had close to forty books in this
series published. Her explanation for this tremendous
volume of superb romance writing is simple: "I love to
write, and it comes very easily to me."

Once Charlotte has begun a story, the plot, the actions
and the personalities of the characters unfold effortlessly
and spontaneously, as her quick fingers commit the ideas
of her fertile imagination to paper.

And so, in her beautiful old home on the rain-swept,
uncrowded Isle of Man, where she lives with her husband
and five children, Charlotte spends eight hours a day at her
typewriter spinning love stories—and enjoying every
minute of it!

Her career as a writer has opened many doors for her,
and travel is one of them. Yet despite all the countries
she has visited and enjoyed in the past few years, her
greatest love is still London, the city where she was
born and raised.

SUPERROMANCE

Longer, exciting, sensual and dramatic!

Fascinating love stories that will hold
you in their magical spell till the last page
is turned!

Now's your chance to discover the earlier
books in this exciting series. Choose from
the great selection on the following page!

Choose from this list of great
SUPERROMANCES!

#1 END OF INNOCENCE   Abra Taylor
The shadow of the bullring turns the love
between Liona and Rafael to hate.

#2 LOVE'S EMERALD FLAME   Willa Lambert
Love flares in the jungle mists, stronger than
danger or fear!

#3 THE MUSIC OF PASSION   Lynda Ward
Driven by her heart's betrayal, Megan seeks
revenge against love.

#4 LOVE BEYOND DESIRE   Rachel Palmer
Pride and deceit refuse what Robin's
heart desires....

#5 CLOUD OVER PARADISE   Abra Taylor
Love's raging passions sweep through a sunlit
Tahitian isle.

#6 SWEET SEDUCTION   Maura Mackenzie
Bound by the past, Denise rejects love — until
passion betrays her!

#7 THE HEART REMEMBERS   Emma Church
Luke and Sara are worlds apart. Can their love
bridge the gap?

#8 BELOVED INTRUDER   Jocelyn Griffin
Destiny throws Penelope and Nigel together...
love forges an unyielding chain!

#9 SWEET DAWN OF DESIRE   Meg Hudson
A tragic memory quenches the fire of
the love between Joy and James.

#10 HEART'S FURY   Lucy Lee
The story of a love more powerful
than the raging North Sea.

SUPERROMANCE

Complete and mail this coupon today!

- -

Worldwide Reader Service

In the U.S.A.
1440 South Priest Drive
Tempe, AZ 85281

In Canada
649 Ontario Street
Stratford, Ontario N5A 6W2

Please send me the following SUPERROMANCES. I am enclosing my check or money order for $2.50 for each copy ordered, plus 75¢ to cover postage and handling.

☐ #1 END OF INNOCENCE
☐ #2 LOVE'S EMERALD FLAME
☐ #3 THE MUSIC OF PASSION
☐ #4 LOVE BEYOND DESIRE
☐ #5 CLOUD OVER PARADISE

☐ #6 SWEET SEDUCTION
☐ #7 THE HEART REMEMBERS
☐ #8 BELOVED INTRUDER
☐ #9 SWEET DAWN OF DESIRE
☐ #10 HEART'S FURY

Number of copies checked @ $2.50 each = $_____
N.Y. and Ariz. residents add appropriate sales tax $_____
Postage and handling $____.75
                                    TOTAL $_____

I enclose_____.
(Please send check or money order. We cannot be responsible for cash sent through the mail.)
Prices subject to change without notice.

NAME_____
              (Please Print)
ADDRESS_____
CITY_____
STATE/PROV._____
ZIP/POSTAL CODE_____
Offer expires June 30, 1982   110562623